SEE THE GAMES AND THE PLAYERS WHO MADE HISTORY!

Here's a lineup for the books—aging and injured players beating the odds, last-place teams surging to victory, rookies playing All-Star ball, runners defying time and gravity. They're all here, part of sports history, playing the games you'll read about again and again: the 1991 World Championship long-jump competition when Carl Lewis made three un_____ 30 foot _____ and Mike Powell, _____ broke the existing _____ Bulls, led by Micha_____ of a "one-man" tea_____ the L.A. Lakers an_____ title, the 1950 Cleveland Browns, who came from behind to upset the Philadelphia Eagles in their first-ever NFL game, and then went on to win the title. . . .

Read all about them—the great teams, the great players, the great games, in . . .

GREAT SPORTS UPSETS 2

Books by Bill Gutman

Sports Illustrated: BASEBALL'S RECORD BREAKERS
Sports Illustrated: GREAT MOMENTS IN BASEBALL
Sports Illustrated: GREAT MOMENTS IN PRO FOOTBALL
Sports Illustrated: PRO FOOTBALL'S RECORD BREAKERS
Sports Illustrated: STRANGE AND AMAZING BASEBALL
  STORIES
Sports Illustrated: STRANGE AND AMAZING FOOTBALL
  STORIES
BASEBALL SUPER TEAMS
BASEBALL'S HOT NEW STARS
BO JACKSON: A BIOGRAPHY
FOOTBALL SUPER TEAMS
GREAT SPORTS UPSETS
GREAT SPORTS UPSETS 2
MICHAEL JORDAN: A BIOGRAPHY
PRO SPORTS CHAMPIONS
STRANGE AND AMAZING WRESTLING STORIES

Available from ARCHWAY Paperbacks

GREAT SPORTS
UPSETS 2

BILL GUTMAN

AN ARCHWAY PAPERBACK
Published by POCKET BOOKS
New York   London   Toronto   Sydney   Tokyo   Singapore

Cover photos: top left, Mike Powell/Allsport; top right, Brian Drake/Sports Chrome, Inc.; bottom left, Focus On Sports; bottom right, Ken Levine/Allsport; back cover: Walter Iooss, Jr./ *Sports Illustrated*.

AN ARCHWAY PAPERBACK *Original*

An Archway Paperback published by
POCKET BOOKS, a division of Simon & Schuster Inc.
1230 Avenue of the Americas, New York, NY 10020

Copyright © 1993 by Bill Gutman

All rights reserved, including the right to reproduce this book or portions thereof in any form whatsoever. For information address Pocket Books, 1230 Avenue of the Americas, New York, NY 10020

ISBN: 0-671-78154-5

First Archway Paperback printing February 1993

10 9 8 7 6 5 4 3 2 1

AN ARCHWAY PAPERBACK and colophon are registered trademarks of Simon & Schuster Inc.

Printed in the U.S.A.

IL 5+

For Cathy

Contents

Introduction

What is it that's so intriguing about a great sports upset? It's not that everyone wants to see it happen, because even in an upset there are a winner and a loser. The upset occurs when an individual or team that was expected to win doesn't. That makes some fans happy; others sad. At the same time, though, most sports fans seem to appreciate and be intrigued by a big upset, especially when the underdog raises the level of his game or sport to new and unexpected heights.

Maybe part of it is America's love of the underdog. When 7′1″ Wilt Chamberlain was dominating National Basketball Association centers and being booed for it, he made a now-famous assessment of the situation.

"Nobody loves Goliath," said Wilt.

He was right. Just like when David slew the giant

Goliath, fans love an underdog who defeats a seemingly superior opponent. There are, of course, upsets and then there are *great* upsets! Great ones are much more dramatic and less likely to occur. So when there is a great upset in sports, it is remembered for years.

When the Cleveland Browns joined the National Football League in 1950, the team was expected to flounder under the pressure of "playing with the big boys." When the New York Giants trailed the Brooklyn Dodgers by 13½ games in mid-August during the 1951 National League pennant race, they were expected to fold up their tents and just play out the string. In both cases, though, it didn't happen the way it should have.

When New York Knicks center Willis Reed severely injured a hip in the fifth game of the 1969–70 NBA finals, everyone figured the L.A. Lakers with the trio of Chamberlain, Elgin Baylor, and Jerry West would romp over the Knicks. Guess again. When Bob Beamon set an incredible long jump record in the 1968 Olympic Games, some thought it could never be broken. Then in the late 1980s and early 1990s, everyone felt that one great track star had a chance to do it. His name was Carl Lewis. At the World Championships in 1991, Lewis had the greatest series of long jumps in track and field history. But it was Mike Powell, with one fantastic jump, who finally defeated Lewis and broke the record.

These are just some of the exciting and unusual stories that are included in *Great Sports Upsets 2*. They are stories of individuals and teams, and of individuals within teams. All surprised the so-called experts, often in spectacular fashion. Between these pages you'll read about the exploits of Paul Brown, Marion Motley, Otto Graham, Bobby Thomson, Len Dawson, Willis Reed, Walt Frazier, Carl Lewis, Mike Powell, Jimmy Connors, Michael Jordan, Scottie Pippen, Jack Morris, Kirby Puckett, and others. All were involved in epic confrontations and epic games that resulted in great sports upsets.

GREAT SPORTS
UPSETS 2

New Kids on the NFL Block

To look back, even now, at what the NFL's Cleveland Browns accomplished in the first decade of their franchise history is mind-boggling. Not only did the Browns dominate professional football, they did it in a way that can never be duplicated. That's because the team played in two leagues with the same spectacular results. When they made the switch from one league to the other, they produced one of the greatest upsets in sports history.

There had been a National Football League team in Cleveland since 1937. They were called the Rams and had many more losing seasons than winning ones. In 1945 the Cleveland Rams finally won the NFL Western Division title with a 9-1 record, then defeated the Washington Redskins, 15–14, in the championship game played on a frozen field in sub-zero weather.

What did the Rams do to celebrate their first NFL title? They moved their franchise from the frozen tundra of Cleveland to the sunny warmth of California and became the Los Angeles Rams. Die-hard football fans back in Cleveland felt betrayed and wondered if they would ever have an NFL team again.

A year later, in 1946, Cleveland found another team, but it wasn't in the NFL. A new professional league called the All-America Football Conference had been formed. There were eight teams, including such long-gone franchises as the New York Yankees, Chicago Rockets, Los Angeles Dons, and Brooklyn Dodgers. There was also a team in Cleveland, and it was called the Browns.

The coach of the Cleveland Browns was named, appropriately, Paul Brown. He would turn out to be an innovative, daring, and great coach. Brown had served a long apprenticeship, beginning when he coached at Massillon High in Ohio. From there he went to Severn Academy, the Great Lakes Naval Training Station, and Ohio State University. When he took over organizing and coaching the professional Browns, he was more than ready.

Brown is often credited with bringing a real sense of team discipline to professional football. He also devised the most intricate forward pass patterns to that time, and he was one of the first pro coaches to freely hire black players. Brown was also adept at hiring the perfect players to execute his precision game plans.

Cleveland dominated the AAC in its first year, finishing with a 12-2 record in the regular season and scoring 423 points while giving up just 137.

They won games by scores of 44–0, 28–0, 51–14, 34–0, and 66–14 among others. Then they won the first-ever AAC championship, defeating the New York Yankees, 14–9.

That would be the first of four straight titles for the Browns. After they won championship number four in 1949, defeating the San Francisco 49ers, 21–7, the entire football world knew about the team that played on the cold and windy wintry shores of Lake Erie. The club had a four-year AAC regular season record of 45-4-3. In 1948 they had a perfect 14-0 mark, then whipped Buffalo, 49–7, for yet another title. This was truly a dominating football team.

The problem was that the All-America Football Conference was not prospering along with the Browns—the league was in big financial trouble. In 1949 negotiations began with the older and more established National Football League. The result was the dissolution of the AAC after the 1949 season. Three of the teams—the Cleveland Browns, San Francisco 49ers, and Baltimore Colts—would be allowed to enter the NFL for the 1950 season.

NFL veterans looked at the three new teams and drooled. Easy wins off them, they felt. These guys would learn what it was to play in a real major league. Both the 49ers and the Colts would find the adjustment difficult. Playing in the Western Division, the 49ers would finish at 3-9 and the Colts at a league worst, 1-11. The Browns would be a different story, a very different story.

Coach Brown had been watching the NFL very closely for a number of years. Maybe he knew all along that only one league could survive. As soon as he learned that the AAC was going to fold and that his team would be allowed into the NFL, he began preparing. He sent two of his coaches—Fritz Heisler and Blanton Collier—to scout the 1949 NFL title game between the Philadelphia Eagles and the Los Angeles Rams. The Eagles won that game, 14–0.

Brown already knew that his team's first NFL game would be against the champion Eagles. He also knew that because they had been AAC champions, all eyes would be on his team. By the time Paul Brown met his team at their first NFL training camp, he had drawn up a master plan to beat the Eagles.

The Browns had a large incentive to win. They knew they represented the best of what had been the AAC. Before the merger someone had once asked a high-ranking NFL official if the two leagues would ever meet.

"Tell them [the AAC] to go get a ball first," the man quipped.

Cleveland not only had a ball, they also had some fine players. Otto Graham was a gifted quarterback, a resourceful passer who knew how to evade a pass rush and get the ball to a receiver. His receivers included two stars, Mac Speedie and Dante Lavelli. Both were able to follow Paul Brown's instructions to a tee.

Marion Motley was one of the first black players in pro ball, a big, strong, pile-driving fullback who had exceptional quickness for his size. Lou "The Toe" Groza was not only an outstanding place-kicker, but a fine tackle as well. Brown had also picked up several other outstanding players from de-

Marion Motley was a fast and powerful fullback for the Browns and one of the first great black players in the NFL. *(Courtesy Cleveland Browns)*

funct AAC teams. They included defensive ends Len Ford and John Kissell, running back Rex Bumgardner, and offensive linemen Abe Gibron and Hal Herring.

Cleveland gave everyone a hint of what was to come by winning all five of its preseason games. Among those victories was a 27–23 triumph over the rough, tough Chicago Bears before more than 51,000 fans at Cleveland. Now the opener with the Eagles was rapidly approaching. Philadelphia had lost several stars because of preseason injuries, including all-star running back Steve Van Buren and offensive tackle Al Wistert. In addition, when the Eagles coaching staff scouted the Browns in preseason, they were surprised by all the new players Brown had picked up from the old AAC.

"Cleveland was not the same team we studied before," said Eagles coach Earle "Greasy" Neale. "They looked more like an AAC all-star team."

Through it all, Paul Brown never stopped experimenting. He put a running back in motion to confuse the defense on pass plays. The Eagles used a 5-4 defense that was great against the run since the tackles plugged the middle and the linebackers came up fast to stop the sweep. It was a defense vulnerable to the pass, though, and Coach Brown felt that gave his club a big advantage.

"There was no way any defensive back could cover our receivers man for man," he said flatly.

Then there was the emotional aspect of an old AAC team playing in the giant NFL. "This was the highest emotional game I ever coached," Paul

6

Brown would say. "We had four years of constant ridicule to get us ready."

Finally it was game time. There was a huge crowd of more than 71,000 fans in Philadelphia to witness this clash of league champions. Despite recent developments, the Eagles were still heavy favorites.

Philadelphia received the opening kickoff and went nowhere. The Browns stopped them three straight times and forced a punt. Cleveland's Don Phelps fielded the punt and suddenly was streaking upfield nearly untouched for an apparent touchdown. The fans were shocked, but the Eagles got a reprieve when the play was called back. Cleveland's Len Ford had been detected clipping. On the same play the Browns lost Lou Groza to a shoulder injury.

None of that really mattered to the Browns. When Graham came out to run the offense, he immediately threw the football so he could check out the Philly defense. All three passes were incomplete, but Graham and Coach Brown had seen what they wanted. The Eagle linebackers were covering the man in motion. That meant Lavelli and Speedie would have only single coverage.

Later, Eagles Coach Neale would say, "We had only the five-four defense. If they beat that, then we didn't have anything to turn to. We were dead."

Philadelphia actually scored first on a 13-yard field goal, but after that Graham and the Browns went to work. Before the first quarter had ended, the QB hit halfback-end Dub Jones on a 59-yard touchdown strike. In the second period it was Dante Lavelli on

7

the receiving end of a 26-yard Graham touchdown aerial. The score was 14–3 at the half. In period number three Mac Speedie got into the act, catching a 12-yard scoring strike from Graham.

The Eagles got a score of their own early in the final period when Pete Pihos caught a 17-yard TD toss from Billy MacKrides. After that it was all Cleveland. Graham had thrown the ball most of the day when Coach Brown suddenly switched to a running game. Motley, Dub Jones, and Bumgardner began chewing up yardage. From the Philly 28, quarterback Graham ran the ball seven straight times (unheard of for a quarterback today) and finally scored from the one.

"We wanted to show them we could run the ball better than they could, too," Graham said later.

A late Cleveland score made the final tally 35–10. Not only had the Browns beaten the Eagles, they had also embarrassed them. Philly lineman Bucko Kilroy returned to the theme of the Browns having a bunch of top ACC players, saying, "We were a good team, but we weren't capable of beating any all-star team tonight."

Another Eagle, Bosh Pritchard, knew the result wasn't a fluke. When his wife asked him what had happened, he replied, "Honey, we just met a team from the big leagues."

The Browns were for real, all right. The headlines screamed what a great upset the game had been. Quarterback Graham had completed 21 of 38 passes for 310 yards and three scores in his first NFL game. When it was over, new NFL Commissioner Bert Bell paid homage to the Browns when he said,

"You have as fine a football team as I've ever seen."

Cleveland wasn't through yet. They proceeded to rip through the NFL schedule, losing only to the New York Giants twice, by scores of 6–0 and 17–13. When they met the Eagles for the second time late in the year, Greasy Neale said Cleveland beat his team the first time only because of Graham's passing. So in the second game the Browns won, 13–7, without throwing a single aerial.

At the end of the season the Browns were tied with the Giants for first in the American Conference with identical 10-2 records. In the National Conference the Rams and Chicago Bears were deadlocked at 9-3. There would be two playoff games before the NFL title game. In the West the Rams beat the Bears, 24–14.

Now the Browns had to face the Giants, the only team that had beaten them all year. Once again the Clevelanders were underdogs, and once again they pulled off an upset. The Browns won the game, 8–3. Most important, just a year after winning their fourth straight AAC title, the team was playing for the NFL championship. No one, except Paul Brown, thought it could happen. Another irony was that the Rams had been the team that moved out of Cleveland, opening the door for the creation of the Browns.

This wouldn't be an easy game, though. Los Angeles had a powerful football team. They were the highest-scoring club in the league, putting 466 points on the board in 12 games. The Browns, by contrast, had scored 310 points. But the Cleveland

9

defense had allowed only 144 points while the Rams let opponents score 309.

There were also many individual stars. The Rams had a pair of outstanding quarterbacks in veteran Bob Waterfield and young Norm Van Brocklin. They often alternated, and between them passed for 3,709 yards, more than 300 a game. That was almost unheard of in 1950. Over one two-week span against the Baltimore Colts and the Green Bay Packers, the Rams scored 70 and 65 points respectively.

Tom Fears, with 84 catches, was the top receiver, but Elroy "Crazy Legs" Hirsch with 42 was the more spectacular receiver to watch. The club had speed runners in Glenn Davis and Verda "Vitamin T" Smith, as well as a power backfield that featured the trio of Paul "Tank" Younger, Dick Hoerner, and "Deacon" Dan Towler. Because of their incredible striking power and established stars, the Rams were favored to win it all. Once again Cleveland was the underdog.

The only major injury was suffered by Ram QB Norm Van Brocklin, who broke some ribs in the playoff game against the Bears. Otherwise, both clubs were ready. The game was played on December 24, 1950. Ironically, it put the Rams back in the place they had left five years earlier. Also, they were playing under the same conditions as five years earlier—a frozen field at Cleveland's huge Municipal Stadium. Surprisingly, just 29,751 fans were on hand to witness this historic clash.

L.A. took the opening kickoff back to its own 18. Knowing Paul Brown was a master strategist, Rams coach Joe Studahar wasted no time in trying some trickery of his own. He decided the Cleveland defense would be concentrating on Fears and Hirsch, with the linebackers keying on running back Smith. On the first play from scrimmage, all three were used as decoys. Both ends and Smith moved to the right. The other back, Glenn Davis, remained in the backfield.

As the Browns' defense moved with Fears, Hirsch, and Smith, Glenn Davis began streaking down the left sideline. Quarterback Waterfield hit him with a perfect pass about midfield, and the former Army All-American blew past Ken Gorgal and Tommy James en route to an 82-yard scoring play. The extra point made it a 7–0 game after just one play and 27 seconds. Maybe the Browns' bubble was finally going to burst?

A lesser team might have been demoralized by the sudden TD strike. Not the Browns. Paul Brown's ballclub never panicked. Starting at its own 28, Cleveland took just six plays to show the Rams what they could do. Graham got 21 yards on several scrambles out of the backfield. The final 32 came on a pass from Graham to Dub Jones. Groza's kick tied the game at 7–7.

Now the two teams settled into a real battle. Before the period ended, the Rams took a 14–7 lead by driving through the Cleveland defense again. Waterfield hit Fears for a 44-yard gain, and Verda Smith ran 15 yards from the 19 to the 4. Then Dick Hoerner ran the ball in for the TD.

At the beginning of the second quarter it was Cleveland's turn. They brought the Rams kickoff

A threat when running or passing the football, Cleveland quarterback Otto Graham was also a clutch performer and outstanding leader—a great football player. *(Courtesy Cleveland Browns)*

back to the 35. After a pass interference call against L.A., Graham threw a completion to Speedie, moving the ball to the Rams' 35. Not one to waste time, Graham went upstairs again and found Dante Lavelli streaking into the end zone. Another score. A bad pass from center caused the

Browns to blow the extra point. It was now 14–13, Rams, with just four minutes gone in the second quarter.

The game to that point had been an offensive explosion, both teams marching up and down the field. Now the defenses began taking over. As the Rams continued to drive deep into Cleveland territory, the Browns defense would rise to the occasion and stop them. On one series of plays, Cleveland's veteran defensive end, Len Ford, who had missed most of the season with a broken jaw, single-handedly pushed the Ram machine backward.

On one play Ford read a reverse and threw Vitamin Smith for a 14-yard loss. On the next play he raced into the backfield and sacked Waterfield to drive the Rams back another 11 yards. Then when L.A. tried a sweep with Glenn Davis, there was Ford again, stripping the blockers and grabbing Davis 13 yards behind the line. At the half the Rams still held a 14–13 lead. The way they were moving the ball, though, it seemed just a matter of time before they broke it wide open.

It was the Browns, however, who drew first blood in the third period. Graham drove his team 77 yards, culminating the march in a 39-yard TD strike to Lavelli. This time Groza converted, and Cleveland had a 20–14 lead. But the Rams didn't score 466 points during the regular season by rolling over and playing dead when they were behind. Midway through the period they began driving again.

A cool and brazen veteran, Bob Waterfield knew how to win. He threw a key 38-yard pass to Smith, coming out of the backfield, who brought the ball

13

to the Cleveland 17. From there Dick Hoerner ran the ball seven straight times at the heart of the Browns' defense. The seventh carry was a fourth-and-goal from the one, and Hoerner slammed into the end zone for the score. Waterfield kicked the extra point, and L.A. had a 21–20 lead.

Next came the kind of break that can simply cause a team to buckle, especially late in a game. The Browns were stopped after a very short kick-off return. Graham then gave the ball to fullback Motley, hoping the big guy would get them some field position. When the Rams swarmed over Motley, the ball squirted loose and began rolling around. Defensive end Larry Brink scooped it up at the six-yard line and ran it into the end zone for another L.A. score, their second in 25 seconds. Waterfield's kick made it 28–20. Shortly after that the third quarter ended. With just 15 minutes remaining, it looked as if the Browns' odyssey was about to end.

Five minutes into the final session the Rams had the ball again. Another touchdown would undoubtedly seal Cleveland's fate. The Rams had worked their way into Browns territory when Waterfield went to the air once more. Only this time Cleveland defensive back Warren Lahr was ready. He intercepted the ball at the 35. Waterfield left dejectedly, and Graham trotted out, clapping his hands and shouting encouragement to his offense.

Paul Brown had wanted Graham from the time he saw him play tailback for Northwestern University. Graham threw just one pass that day, but the wily coach recognized a great talent. When a game was on the line, Graham was always at his best. Against the Rams in the fourth period he began demonstrating that quality once more.

He drove his team upfield slowly. At one point he was faced with a fourth-and-four situation and calmly passed seven yards for a first down. On another fourth-down play he scrambled for a first. Yet at one point in the drive, he also completed five passes in a row. Finally, with the ball at the L.A. 14, Graham dropped back and hit Rex Bumgardner in the end zone for the score. Groza's kick reduced the L.A. margin to one at 28–27.

The Browns' defense wouldn't allow the Rams to move again. Four plays later the Browns had the ball back, and Graham moved the team into Rams territory once more. Cleveland was near the 30-yard line, well within field goal range for Groza. Graham wanted more. He tried to run it himself and, after getting a first down, was blindsided by Milan Lazetich and fumbled the ball back to L.A.

"I never saw him coming," Graham said later. "What I wanted to do was dig a hole in the middle of the field and crawl into it. But when I reached the sidelines, Paul [Coach Brown] put his arm around my shoulder and said, 'Don't worry. You'll get another chance, and we'll win this thing yet.'"

One first down and the Rams might have run out the clock, but the Browns stopped Hoerner twice for no gain, then nailed Davis after a gain of six. Now Waterfield had to punt again. There were two minutes left when he boomed a 51-yarder that Cliff

Lewis grabbed at the 19. He lugged it back to the Cleveland 32. With 1:50 left on the clock, the Browns were 68 yards from the end zone and maybe 30 to 35 yards from field goal range.

Once again Otto Graham took the game into his own hands. First he ran 19 yards to the Rams 49. Then he fired a 10-yard completion to Bumgardner at the 39. Seconds later he hit two more clutch passes, first to Jones, then to Bumgardner again. Now the ball was at the 11, and Lou Groza was warming up his famous toe. Graham called a timeout.

Browns assistant coach Blanton Collier remembered the ball being placed on the left hashmark. There was a brisk right-to-left crosswind blowing. Coach Brown called Collier, who was up in the press box, and asked for his opinion. Kick now or run one more play?

"I suggested he let Otto run a sneak to the right because of the wind," Collier said. "Then kick it on the next play. Paul said okay and hung up the phone. I remember it dawning on me right away that I must be crazy, to take a chance running another play and risking a fumble on that frozen ground, just to get a yard or two and a better angle. I tell you, I must have lived a hundred years in the next few seconds as Otto ran the play."

But Graham was flawless. He sneaked the ball another yard while moving it closer to the center of the field. Now Groza got ready to try a 16-yard field goal, the most important kick of his career.

"The only thing I thought about was my own checklist for kicking the ball," Groza remembered. "I didn't hear the crowd, I blotted out the distance,

Lou "The Toe" Groza was a Hall of Fame kicker and also a fine tackle for the Browns. His clutch field goal in the final seconds enabled his club to win the NFL title their first year in the league. *(Courtesy Cleveland Browns)*

the time on the clock, and even the score. All I concentrated on was kicking the ball.''

Center Hal Herring snapped the ball to holder Tommy James. James placed it on the frozen turf as Groza stepped into it, swinging his right left in a short but powerful arc. The ball sailed up over the Ram defenders and through the uprights. IT WAS GOOD!

The historic moment was captured on film by photographers. Players didn't wear face masks in those days, and as soon as Groza kicked it, all heads turned toward the goalposts. Both the Rams and Browns players, standing together, looked as if they were frozen in time.

Seconds later the stadium erupted. Groza's kick had given the Browns a 30–28 lead with just 28 seconds left. It was too much for the Rams to overcome. Cleveland had done it. They had won the championship and in doing so had provided one of the great upsets in sports history.

Everyone thought the Browns would get their comeuppance when they joined the NFL. After all, these were the big boys, and the Clevelanders were coming from a league that had existed only four years. But Paul Brown, Otto Graham, and the rest of the Browns had talent, pride and a burning desire to win, and they came to the NFL with something to prove. Under pressure all year long, the team continued to fight and persevere. They ended up with the title.

The Browns saga didn't end there. They went on to win five consecutive divisional titles, six in the next seven years, taking two more NFL crowns during that time. Counting their four years of domination in the All-American Football Conference, the Cleveland Browns had a football dynasty that lasted for more than a decade. But despite their overall success, it's that first NFL title in 1950 that's remembered most. That was the one no one thought they had a chance to win.

The Shot Heard Round the World

Almost every baseball fan knows about "The Shot Heard Round the World." It is the name given to one of the most famous and dramatic home runs in baseball history. It was hit by Bobby Thomson of the old *New York* Giants off Ralph Branca of the old *Brooklyn* Dodgers. It won the 1951 pennant for the Giants.

What some people forget is the entire story of that epic pennant race. When it started, the Dodgers were considered the best team by far in the National League. They had it all, powerful hitting and outstanding pitching, a ballclub led by a quartet of future Hall of Famers. When the Brooks opened up a 13½-game lead over the second-place Giants in mid-August, the pennant race seemed all but over. But what happened over the final six weeks in the season is still considered one of the greatest upsets in baseball history.

The Dodgers were close to being a National League dynasty from the late 1940s right through the mid-1950s. Brooklyn won pennants in 1947, '49, '52, '53, and '55. They were a close second in three of the other four seasons. The team was a powerhouse. The infield featured Gil Hodges at first, Jackie Robinson at second, Harold "Pee Wee" Reese at short, and Billy Cox at third. Roy Campanella was the catcher, while Edwin "Duke" Snider and Carl Furillo were stars in the outfield. Don Newcombe, Preacher Roe, Carl Erskine, and Ralph Branca formed a solid quartet of starting pitchers. This was a team that could do it all.

Playing in the cozy confines of Ebbets Field made the Dodgers even better. The fans in Brooklyn loved their team and hated the opposition. There was a runway leading from the field to the clubhouse that enemy players had to pass through. Dodgers fans would often pelt the opposition with cups, food, beer, and anything else they could get their hands on. Walking through that runway was the same as running the gauntlet.

Back in 1951 there were three major league baseball teams in New York. The American League had the Yankees, the perennial world champs and bitter rivals of the Dodgers. An even more bitter rival of the Dodgers was the National League New York Giants. Whenever the Dodgers and Giants met, it was war. It had been like that for decades.

Whitey Lockman, who played first base for the

'51 Giants, remembers the feeling whenever the two teams met.

"The atmosphere was always electric," Lockman said. "It was war whenever we met, maybe even more so in Ebbets Field than in our park, the Polo Grounds. Everything was so close at Ebbets, and the fans were more emotional. There was just something special about the games we played against the Dodgers."

By 1951 the rivalry had become more intense. That was because the Giants' manager then was the fiery Leo Durocher. Known as Leo the Lip, Durocher had successfully managed the Dodgers for a decade. Then, in the middle of the 1948 season, Durocher changed teams, going from the Dodgers to the Giants in one day. When he met with his new team for the first time, Durocher ran his hand across the front of his chest and said one word—

"Giants!"

He was telling the team that he was now a Giant and that was the only thing that mattered. Leo Durocher's one loyalty was to winning. He was intensely competitive and would do anything to win, even if it meant making enemies. He spent the next three years remaking the Giants, bringing in new players and making several trades. A key move was a deal with the Braves that brought shortstop Alvin Dark and second-sacker Eddie Stanky to the Giants.

Durocher had been a player with the scrappy St. Louis Cardinals Gas House Gang, world champs in 1934, and he always wanted the same kind of hustling, fighting players around him. Scratchers and divers, he called them. By 1951 he felt the Giants were ready and predicted they would beat the Dodgers and win the pennant.

At the beginning of the season the Giants were playing Monte Irvin at first, Stanky at second, Dark at short, with Henry Thompson at third. Whitey Lockman was in left, Bobby Thomson in center, and Don Mueller in right. Wes Westrum was the catcher and a great handler of pitchers. The pitching staff was led by a trio of right-handers, the crafty Sal "The Barber" Maglie, who had learned his trade in the outlaw Mexican League, Larry Jansen, and Jim Hearn. Dave Koslo and Sheldon Jones were other starters, with George Spencer a valuable arm out of the bullpen.

Durocher called these Giants "my kind of team," but you wouldn't know it the way the season started. The ballclub won two of its first three games, then promptly went into a tailspin and lost 11 straight games. A 2-12 start is not a record that wins pennants. Their archrivals, the Dodgers, were at 8-4 and already taunting the Giants through the clubhouse door at Ebbets Field.

The Giants just weren't hitting. Bobby Thomson was at .193, Lockman at .200, Mueller at .216, and Irvin at .245. Meanwhile, the Dodger stars were busting the ball all over the place. This made Dodger manager Charley Dressen very happy. Dressen was an astute baseball man who had once coached under Durocher. Leo had called him "my right arm." Now that they were rivals, Dressen wanted nothing more than to beat his former boss.

Durocher shook up the lineup, and the Giants finally broke their losing streak with an 8–5 win over the Dodgers. Most observers felt the pennant race was all but over for them, though.

"It would take a miracle for the Giants to win the championship now," wrote columnist Arthur Daley. "The losing streak represents a far greater disaster than the faltering start a year ago. . . . The Dodger power hitting can dominate the pennant race as it hasn't been dominated in decades."

Durocher rarely berated his players. He encouraged them, boosted them up. Sure, he would yell and scream if someone made a mistake. Once he had his say, though, it was forgotten. He never cut his players down to the press. If things weren't going well, he always looked to shake things up.

"Leo was never a guy to stand pat," said Bobby Thomson. "Change, change, change, change. That was Leo's way. His theory was 'Let's not sit in this rut. Let's try something different, anything different.' "

By May 24 the Giants had worked their way up to 17-19, but still trailed the 20-13 Dodgers by 4½ games. Though they weren't yet at the .500 mark, the Giants were 15-7 since the 11-game losing streak. They were playing much better, but Durocher wasn't satisfied. He decided to make a bold move. He convinced team owner Horace Stoneham to call up a 20-year-old center fielder from the team's Minneapolis farm club. The kid was hitting a scorching .477 for the Millers and had the look of a superstar. His name—Willie Mays.

Mays could do it all—hit, run, throw, steal bases, and hit with power. When he joined the team, Durocher made some other moves. Monte Irvin was

This is the great Willie Mays during his later years with the Giants, after the team moved to San Francisco. In 1951, Mays was the rookie who sparked the *New York* Giants and helped them to a miracle pennant. *(Courtesy San Francisco Giants)*

struggling at first, his play in the field affecting his hitting. So the manager moved him to left and brought Lockman in to play first. Lockman proved a natural at the position and picked it up quickly. Mays had to play center, so Bobby Thomson became the odd man out for a few weeks, playing some left, some right, and pinch hitting. But he would later settle in at third base and provide some unexpected spark in an unfamiliar position.

What some fans also tend to forget about 1951 is that it was just four years since Jackie Robinson had become the first black player in the big leagues. Jackie joined the Dodgers in 1947 and went through a very difficult period his first year because he had promised Dodger president Branch Rickey that he would turn the other cheek to any abuses and taunts.

Jackie was talented and combative, a player who refused to lose. He quickly became a Dodger mainstay and was followed to Brooklyn by catcher Campanella and pitcher Newcombe, two more outstanding black players. Mays would join Irvin, Henry Thompson, and backup catcher Ray Noble as black players on the Giants. Yet even in 1951 there was only one other black player among the six other National League teams. He was Sam Jethroe of the Braves. So these first black players were under a lot of pressure to perform. There was still a lot of discrimination, especially with housing and places to eat.

"I think that kind of thing gave us more determination," Don Newcombe has said. "We were angry and the only way we could vent that anger was on the ballfield. Because of that, we'd come to the ballpark with a decided edge. . . . So we excelled because we were black. We had the need to excel, to show people we were as good or better."

Mays was also expected to excel. He was a muscular 5'11" 170-pounder who loved baseball and brought a boyish enthusiasm and his own style to the game. (He would often lose his cap when running hard and catch routine fly balls basket-style, at his waist.) He also had the instinct and daring to make the great catch and had a cannon for a throwing arm.

The early problem was his hitting. Willie went hitless in his first 12 trips to the plate. He felt he couldn't hit big-league pitching and asked Durocher to return him to Minneapolis. The manager put his arm around the rookie's shoulder and said, "Willie, I brought you up here for one reason. To play center field. You're the best center fielder I've ever seen, and you're gonna be out there tomorrow, next week, and next month. Just play center for me and don't worry about the hits."

One night later Mays got his first big-league hit. It was a long home run against the great left-hander Warren Spahn of the Braves. Finally it looked as if Mays and the Giants were on the way. By the end of June the club was in second place at 38-31, trailing the 41-25 Dodgers by 4½ games. A month later, on July 31, the Giants had moved to 55-44, but the Dodgers were playing very well and at 62-32 seemed unbeatable. They led the Giants by 7½ games and seemed to be ready to break the race wide open.

The Giants were now playing solid baseball. Bobby Thomson had moved to third base and was finally hitting with power and consistency. Once he moved to left field, Monte Irvin began putting together a great season and was up among the leaders in runs batted in. Mays was now living up to his advance billing. He had his average up and was tied with Thomson for the club lead with 17 home runs. He was also playing brilliantly in the field. Maglie, Jansen, and Hearn were all pitching well.

The Dodgers still looked unbeatable, though. Hodges, Snider, and Campanella were all genuine sluggers. Robinson and Furillo were outstanding hitters. Reese was a brilliant shortstop and base runner, the glue that held the team together. In fact, Duke Snider always felt the 1951 Dodgers were one of the greatest teams of all time. In early August they were playing that way. They slowly lengthened their lead. Then on August 8 the Giants came in to Ebbets Field for a day-night doubleheader, followed by a single game the next day.

The Dodgers took the twin bill by scores of 7–2 and 7–6. Then the next day they swept the series with a 6–5 victory. The Giants were now 59-50 and the Dodgers 69-35. Brooklyn had a 12½-game lead. In the eyes of everyone the pennant race ended right then and there. It would take more than an upset for the Giants to win. It would take a miracle.

Even the Dodgers felt that way. At Ebbets Field only a thin wooden door separated the two locker rooms. After the 6–5 victory to ensure the sweep, manager Dressen encouraged several of the Dodgers to give the Giants the business. A number of them walked up to the door and began banging their bats against it. Then they began shouting.

"The Giants are dead! The Giants are dead! How do you like it now, Leo!"

Inside the Giant locker room there was growing anger. The taunts continued. Several Dodgers began singing to the tune of "Roll Out the Barrel."

"Roll out the barrel, we got the Giants on the run!"

They repeated this for several more minutes, and in those few moments alone the face of the 1951 pennant race may have changed. Some of the Giants remembered their reactions. Utility infielder Bill Rigney recalls the incident vividly.

"We all knew they had buried us by sweeping the series," Rigney said. "Because they had beaten us so badly, we had to sit there and take it. But we didn't forget it. We knew who was singing."

Giant captain Alvin Dark took it even one step further. "Human beings can only take so much, and we had a bellyful," Dark recalled. "You just can't treat human beings like they treated us and get away with it."

Rookie pitcher Clem Labine, who had joined the Dodgers just two weeks before the incident, couldn't believe what he heard that day.

"I don't care what other people say, that had to be the worst thing that ever happened to us," Labine remembered. "A lot of us were saying, shut up, leave them alone."

After the game some members of the press asked Manager Durocher if he planned to shake up his team again, make changes. After all, that was his style. But this time Durocher fooled them. He gave his team the ultimate backing, and in a voice loud enough for them to hear.

"This is my team," he said. "There will be no changes in the lineup. If they go down, I go down with them. If they go up, so do I. This is my team and I'm going to stick with it."

Ernie Harwell was a Giants broadcaster in 1951. He, too, remembers the incident and Dressen's *The Giants is* [sic] *dead!* comment appearing in all the newspapers and being talked about on the radio.

"It [Dressen's comment] seared itself into the Giant players' brains," said Harwell. "But they didn't run off half-cocked. Leo Durocher was a master psychologist and kept his players relaxed, but effective."

Then on August 11 the Giants returned to the Polo Grounds and were shut out by Robin Roberts and the Phils, 4–0. At the same time the Dodgers won the first game of their doubleheader from the Braves, 8–1, as Ralph Branca upped his record to 10-3. At that precise moment the Dodgers led the Giants by 13½ games, a number that is remembered symbolically to this day. Boston won the second game, 8–4, so at the end of the day Brooklyn had a 13-game lead.

That set the stage for perhaps the most dramatic final six weeks in baseball history. It would have been hard, at that point, to find anyone who felt the Giants could still win. Even if the team got red hot, it was impossible to think of this powerful Dodger ballclub collapsing.

Then the Giants began to win. One, two, three straight. Then three more. When they won their seventh in a row, it was the club's longest winning streak of the year. They had also pared five games off the Brooklyn lead. It was now down to 8 games.

"We had decided to play it one game at a time," Durocher said. "After each game I just gave them a short talk in the clubhouse, tell them they were playing great and to go home and get a good night's sleep. I told them not to worry about anything, to just keep playing the way they had been playing. But I never told them we were going to win it. But after the streak reached 10, then 11, I found myself saying, 'Hey, this club *can* win it.' ''

On August 27 the Giants beat the Cubs in a doubleheader to run their winning streak to 16 games. That same day the Dodgers split with the Braves. Now the Giants were at 75-51. The Dodgers, who had gone 9-9 during the Giants win streak, had a 79-45 record. The gap between the two ballclubs had been reduced to 5 games. Suddenly there was a pennant race. Just two weeks earlier there had been nothing but a rout.

For the next two weeks it was almost a standoff. The lead stayed between 5 and 7 games. The Dodgers were getting some unexpected mound help from young Labine, who won his first four starts. The Giants had gotten a similar lift from lefty Al Corwin a bit earlier in the season. In early September the Giants topped the Dodgers twice, 8–1 and 11–2, cutting the lead to five once again. They had also won five straight over Brooklyn. It took until September 16 for the Giants to finally get it under five. Two days later the lead was down to a scant three games. Now it really was a dogfight.

Finally it came down to the wire. The Giants continued to chip away at the Dodger lead. It was a mere half game when the Dodgers met the Phils on September 28. The Dodgers had a 3–1 lead in the last of the eighth, but Philly's Andy Seminick belted a two-run homer off Carl Erskine to tie it. Then in the bottom of the ninth Willie Jones drove home Richie Ashburn with the winning run. The Dodgers were beaten, 4–3, but more important, their almost season-long lead was gone. They were tied with the Giants at 94-58 each. Now there were just two games left in the regular season.

As it turned out, both teams won their final two games, the Giants beating the Braves and the Dodgers topping the Phils. But in their final game with the Phillies, the Dodgers were saved by Jackie Robinson. The man who refused to lose made a diving catch in the 12th inning for the third out with the winning run on third. Then, in the 14th, he belted a long home run to win it. Both clubs finished the regular season tied at 96-58. They would now have to meet each other in a best-of-three playoff to determine the National League champion.

What a finish it had been for the Giants. They had won 37 of their final 44 games, ending the year with 12 of their last 13 and seven in a row. The Dodgers won only six of their final 13. If they could have squeezed out just one more victory, the race would have been over.

There had been only one best-of-three playoff in the National League up to this time. In 1946 the St. Louis Cardinals had beaten the Dodgers two straight when the Dodgers chose to open the playoffs in St. Louis and found themselves fatigued by a 22-hour train ride (teams didn't travel by plane then). Now the Dodgers won the toss again. They opted to open at Ebbets Field, where they had beaten the Giants 9 times in 11 tries so far. The second and third games (if a third was necessary) would be at the Polo Grounds.

Jim Hearn with a 16-9 record squared off against Ralph Branca, who was 13-10 but with five straight losses, in the first game. Hearn had a strained ligament in his left side, but he didn't tell Durocher. He just had the trainer rub it down with a hot salve. Baseball was a different kind of game back then.

"Jim and I drove to the ballpark together that day," catcher Wes Westrum recalled. "During the entire ride we talked about how to pitch the Dodgers and what we would do in certain situations. I knew Jim had a pull in his side, and we agreed not to tell Leo. You simply played hurt back then."

With 30,707 screaming fans jammed into tiny Ebbets Field, Jim Hearn was next to brilliant. He tossed a five-hitter and got home run support from Bobby Thomson and Monte Irvin. The Giants won the game, 3–1, defeating Branca and putting the Dodgers' backs squarely up against the wall. For now the playoffs would return to the Polo Grounds.

Manager Dressen made a strange pitching choice in the second game. He went to the rookie Clem Labine. It was strange because Labine had been so brilliant after being brought up in August, winning four straight. But one bad pitch against the Phils put him in Dressen's doghouse, and he pitched only once in relief the final 10 days of the season. Many still feel that if Dressen had not taken Labine out of the rotation, the Dodgers would have won it.

Before Game Two the young right-hander remembered wanting the ball. "I can recall feeling pressure, but it was a nice pressure," Labine said. "If you like to play the game, it's the kind of pressure you like. You want the ball. That's how I felt on October 2. I wanted to pitch that game.''

Pitch he did. Durocher decided to rest both Sal Maglie and Larry Jansen, holding them for a possible third game. He went, instead, with Sheldon Jones, and the Dodgers jumped all over him. It was a laugher, the final score being 10–0 with young Labine pitching a six-hitter. Now the National League pennant rested on one final game.

It was a warm Indian-summer day on October 3, 1951. Surprisingly, there were just 34,320 fans at the ancient Polo Grounds. Some 20,000 seats were empty. With a bitter rivalry and the pennant at stake, it was hard to believe. Sal Maglie, with a brilliant 23-6 record, was set to face Dodger Don Newcombe, who was 20-9. Both pitchers were tired from the long season.

Maglie was shaky in the first inning, and the Dodgers jumped to a 1–0 lead, with Jackie Robinson driving the run home with a base hit. Newcombe had his good fastball working and buzzed through the Giants in the first inning. He felt good.

A base-running mistake by Bobby Thomson cut short a Giant threat in the second, and then both pitchers settled down. It was still a 1–0 game through the fifth and sixth. Then in the bottom of the seventh, the Giants got something going. Monte Irvin, who would lead the league with 121 RBIs that year, started it off with a double to left. Lockman was next and bunted. The Dodgers didn't play the ball well, and both runners were safe, Lockman on first and Irvin on third.

Now Bobby Thomson was up. The Flying Scot, as he was called, had been a hot hitter the entire second half of the season. He already had 31 homers and 97 RBIs. Now he dug in. With the count 0-2, Thomson went after a hard slider away and hit a fly ball to medium center. Snider grabbed it, but Irvin tagged and came home with the tying run. Once again the Giants were coming from behind.

In the eighth, however, Maglie suddenly lost it. One-out hits by Reese and Snider put runners on first and third. A wild pitch allowed Pee Wee to score, making it 2-1. Robinson was then walked intentionally, setting up a possible double play. Andy Pafko was next. He hit a tricky hopper toward third. Thomson went to backhand it, wanting to step on third to force Snider. The ball glanced off his mitt, and Snider came home with the third Dodger run, Robinson hustling to third.

After Hodges struck out, Billy Cox slammed a Maglie curve toward third. This one skipped past Thomson into left for a hit. Robinson scored the fourth Dodger run of the game. Maglie retired Rube Walker for the third out, but the Dodgers had suddenly taken a 4-1 lead, and the Giants had just six outs left. Once again they were on the brink of defeat.

They could do nothing with Newcombe in the eighth. Larry Jansen pitched the top of the ninth for the Giants and retired the Dodgers. Now the Giants came up for one last chance, still trailing 4-1. As the team got ready to hit, Manager Durocher began to head out to the third-base coaching lines. Suddenly he turned and said, "Boys, you've come this far. Let's give 'em a finish."

Captain Al Dark was the first up. He felt the same as every member of the Giants team. "If we didn't quit the last six weeks, we certainly weren't going to quit in the last inning of the last game."

Dark slapped a grounder between first and second for a base hit. The ball ticked off Hodges's mitt and just skipped past the lunging Robinson. Don Mueller was next, and he, too, slapped a single between first and second. Now there were two men on with none out and Monte Irvin due up. Irvin was the Giants' best hitter.

Irvin knew a homer would tie the game, and he tried to pull an outside slider. The result was a pop to first. One out. Now Whitey Lockman was up, and he was thinking the same thing. But he wasn't as powerful a hitter as Irvin. "I wouldn't try to pull the outside pitch," he said.

Good thing, because Newcombe worked him outside and Lockman went with it, sending a liner over third and into the left field corner. Dark came around to score, and Lockman headed for second. Mueller, coming into third, hesitated about sliding. He caught his spikes and suffered a painful ankle injury. It was now a 4–2 game, but with Mueller rolling on the ground in pain, the tension was broken, especially for the next hitter, Bobby Thomson.

"I was so concerned about Don, who was not only a teammate but a good friend, that I forgot about the game situation," said Bobby. "I just hustled down to third to see if Don was all right."

While the Giants gathered around their teammate,

the Dodgers made a pitching change. Manager Dressen called Ralph Branca into the game and to a date with baseball history.

"I don't remember anything from the time I left the bull pen until I got to the dirt of the infield," Branca recalled. "It's just a blank. Then I remember seeing Jackie and Pee Wee."

Branca took his warmup tosses as Mueller was removed from the field on a stretcher. As Thomson began walking back toward the plate, Manager Durocher put his arm around him.

"Bobby," he said, "if you ever hit one, hit one now."

Thomson looked at his skipper and thought to himself, "Leo, you're out of your mind."

Then he dug in. On deck was Willie Mays, a very nervous rookie who was hoping he wouldn't have to hit. But now it was Thomson and Branca, just the two of them focusing on the task at hand.

"Once I realized Branca was in the game, there were no other thoughts in my head," Bobby said. "The game situation was no longer on my mind. It was just total concentration on the ball. I just kept telling myself to wait and watch, wait and watch."

Branca wanted to get ahead in the count and fired a fastball right down the middle. Thomson took it. Strike one.

"I nearly fell off the bench when he took that one for a strike," Larry Jansen would say later. On the mound Branca thought about his pitching sequence. He wanted the second pitch to be up and in, to back Bobby off the plate a little. Then he would come back with the low outside curve on the third pitch. The big righty got set and threw.

The ball was up and in, but not as far up or as far in as Branca wanted it. Thomson sprung out of his crouch and lashed at the inside pitch. The crack of the bat could be heard throughout the old ballpark. Suddenly everyone was on his feet. Perhaps the best way to describe what happened next is to recall the words of Giant announcer Russ Hodges, who was high above the field in the radio booth.

Said Hodges, "There's a long fly . . . it's gonna be . . . I believe . . ." Then he paused for a split second before erupting in shouts of glee, *"The Giants win the pennant! The Giants win the pennant! The Giants win the pennant! The Giants win the pennant!"*

Hodges screamed the words four times. Bobby Thomson, indeed, had taken Branca's pitch into the lower-left-field seats for a three-run, game-winning and pennant-winning homer. It would become the Shot Heard Round the World, one of the most famous and remembered home runs in baseball history.

But it was more than that. It also culminated one of the greatest pennant races ever between the most intense rivals the baseball world has ever seen. On top of that, the home run capped the most improbable comeback ever. The Giants had been written off from the time of that 11-game losing streak at the beginning of the season. Yet they rallied around their manager, kept playing, chased the Dodgers down, and caught them.

Thomson was the hero; Branca the goat. Today the two men are good friends and enjoy reliving one

After Bobby Thomson hit his pennant-winning homer, the Giants celebrated wildly in their locker room. Here Thomson is flanked by teammate Whitey Lockman (left) and Giants owner Horace Stoneham. *(Courtesy Bobby Thomson)*

of baseball's most dramatic moments. Back then, though, it was an incredible final six weeks and an even more amazing moment.

"The Dodgers may have had the best team over the long haul," Whitey Lockman would say. "But during those last six weeks we were the better team."

Jackie Robinson had another, more simple explanation. "The Giants caught lightning in a bottle," Robby said.

Either way, it was one of the greatest upsets the diamond world had ever seen.

The AFL Comes of Age

In August of 1959 Lamar Hunt announced to the world the creation of a second professional football league. Hunt said it would be called the American Football League and begin play the following year, 1960. Right away the officials of the established National Football League scoffed. Not another new league, they said. After all it was only 14 years earlier that the All-America Football Conference started, lasting only four seasons.

But Lamar Hunt was well organized and had solid financial backing. He felt that professional sports was on the verge of a new era and that there would be plenty of room for another league. ABC television apparently agreed. In June of 1960 the TV network signed a five-year contract to air AFL games. With eight teams set to go, the new league was about to become a reality.

Ironically, Hunt of Dallas and Bud Adams of Houston wanted to place expansion teams in the NFL. When they were turned down, they opted to form the new league. The original eight teams were in Houston, New York, Buffalo, Boston, Los Angeles, Dallas, Oakland, and Denver. The NFL in 1960 had just expanded from 12 to 13 teams with the debut of the Dallas Cowboys. Plans were already under-way to add the Minnesota Vikings in 1961. NFL people still didn't feel the new league would last.

It was difficult in those early years. Some of the AFL teams were playing in college stadiums. Poor attendance plagued others. In addition, the quality of the football wasn't top-notch. Many of the players in the early AFL years were former NFL veterans, coming back for a last hurrah—castoffs who couldn't quite make it in the NFL and marginal players. What the league emphasized, however, was a wide-open passing game.

Houston was the first AFL champ, and the Oilers had former NFLer George Blanda doing the throwing. A year later Blanda threw for 3,330 yards and 36 touchdowns. In 1963 the Dallas Texans moved to Kansas City and were renamed the Chiefs. The floundering New York Titans were purchased by a syndicate headed by Sonny Werblin and renamed the Jets. The San Diego Chargers had an explosive offensive team led by running backs Keith Lincoln and Paul Lowe, and a wide receiver named Lance Alworth, who was so talented he could play in any league.

Things were beginning to stabilize, and within a year there were more indications that the AFL was here to stay. The league signed a new five-year, $36-million TV contract with ABC. And shortly afterward the New York Jets signed a young quarterback out of Alabama to a huge contract. When Joe Namath put his signature to a $400,000 deal, the face of all sports was changed forever.

The signing of Joe Namath escalated the bidding war for talent among the two leagues. Both realized that something had to be done to keep signing bonuses and contracts from going through the roof. Then the AFL took the price war one step further in 1966 and dropped an agreement that said neither league would sign players from the other's rosters. It was close to outright war.

That was when a series of meetings resolved things. It was decided that the now nine AFL teams would join the now 15 NFL teams in a complete merger by 1970. As a precursor to the complete merger, it was decided that starting at the end of the 1966 season, the champions of both leagues would meet in a special world championship game. It was Lamar Hunt who came up with a name for this new game. He got the idea from his young daughter. He saw her playing with a ball one day and asked what it was.

"This is my super ball," she said.

Hunt simply changed two letters and named the new game the Super Bowl. Though the full merger was still several years away, the NFL was anxious for the Super Bowl to prove just how superior their game was to that of the AFL. In the first Super Bowl ever, Vince Lombardi's Green Bay Packers defeated Hank Stram's Kansas City Chiefs, 35–10.

The Packers, of course, were the greatest team of their era. They made it look easy.

A year later, following the 1967 season, the Packers did it again. They won Super Bowl II by topping the Oakland Raiders, 33–14. Still no question of which team was the best, but AFL people kept insisting that their league was close to or had achieved parity with the NFL. In other words, they were just as good. Prove it, said NFL purists.

In Super Bowl III they did. The New York Jets, led by their $400,000 quarterback, Joe Namath, pulled off an incredible upset when they topped the powerful Baltimore Colts, 16–7. The Colts had been 13-1 in the regular season and were considered the NFL's best in 1967. Yet Namath had brashly "guaranteed" the victory that he and his teammates delivered.

So as the 1969 season got under way, both leagues recognized its significance. For one thing, it was the final season before the merger that would put all the teams in a reorganized National Football League. The AFL teams wanted to make the last year of their old identity a memorable one. What better way than to win Super Bowl IV, making it two in a row for their supposedly inferior league. That would show everyone that the merger was between two very equal leagues.

On the other hand, the old NFLers still believed that the Jets victory over the Colts was a fluke. Their league on the whole, they felt, still played superior football. They would prove it in Super Bowl IV, no matter which team represented them.

In the eyes of many the Oakland Raiders were

the class of the AFL. The Raiders proved it in the regular season finishing at 12-1-1 to win the Western Division title. The Chiefs finished second at 11-3. In the East the Jets were trying to defend their championship and won the division at 10-4. Because of the NFL playoff schedule, the AFL added an extra week and devised a one-year crossover system. The Eastern champion Jets had to play the second place Western Chiefs, while the Raiders would meet the Houston Oilers, second in the East. The two survivors would play for the last-ever AFL crown.

First the Chiefs upset the Jets, 13–6, while the Raiders wiped out the Oilers, 56–7. A week later Kansas City upset Oakland in the league title game, 17–7, as their fine defense dominated the action. Great, snickered NFL fans. Now our champion will have to play a second-place team.

The NFL champion in 1969 was the Minnesota Vikings. The Vikes had been 12-2 during the regular season, led by a defense that yielded a pro football low of just 133 points in 14 games. In the conference championships, the Vikings defeated the Los Angeles Rams, 23–20, then bounced back to win the NFL title easily over the Cleveland Browns, 23–7. So it would be the Vikings, an expansion team back in 1961, meeting the Chiefs in Super Bowl IV. As it was the year before, the National Football League team was a heavy favorite.

Why not? The Vikings had scored the most points while giving up the fewest in the entire league. The sometimes awkward but highly effective Joe Kapp was the quarterback. Rough and tumble, Kapp was a real leader. While not a picture passer, he got the

44

job done. His toughness was already legendary. In a game against Cleveland he slammed directly into Browns linebacker Jim Houston, knocking him out cold.

"Other quarterbacks run out of bounds," said Vikings coach Bud Grant. "Kapp turns upfield and looks for a tackle to run into."

His running backs, halfback Dave Osborn and fullback Bill Brown, were both grind-it-out guys who liked to get their uniforms dirty. Wide receivers Gene Washington and John Henderson and tight end John Beasley were good, but not great. The offensive line, led by the likes of Jim Vellone, Mick Tingelhoff, and Ron Yary, was undeniably one of the best.

But it was the defense that formed the heart and soul of the team. The front four were nicknamed the "Purple People Eaters." Ends Carl Eller and Jim Marshall and tackles Alan Page and Gary Larsen were all outstanding. Page and Eller were perennial all-pros. Linebackers Roy Winston, Lonny Warwick, and Wally Hilgenberg were very solid. The secondary of Earsell Mackbee, Ed Sharockman, Karl Kassulke, and Paul Krause was an outstanding unit that could both hit and go after the football.

The Chiefs had been an outstanding AFL team since 1966, the year they won the league title and played in Super Bowl I. This was a big, strong ballclub not unlike the Vikings, especially in the trenches. Many felt that the Chiefs could be even more explosive than Minnesota offensively. Coach Hank Stram used a play-action offense, his quarterback faking to his runners before dropping back to pass. Stram also used something he called the "moving pocket," in which both the quarterback and his blockers moved to the right or left together. Stram felt his system was innovative and labeled his attack "the offense of the seventies."

He seemed to have found the right quarterback to run things. Len Dawson was a former All-American from Purdue who never really got a chance to show his stuff in the NFL. He had brief trials with both the Cleveland Browns and Pittsburgh Steelers, but was cut both times. When he joined the Chiefs, Dawson proved an able leader and an extremely accurate passer. He was a fine professional quarterback and acquitted himself well in Super Bowl I, completing 16 of 27 passes for 211 yards, one touchdown, and one interception against Green Bay. So he already had Super Bowl experience. In addition, he had thrown 192 touchdown passes in his eight years with the Chiefs. No quarterback in either league had thrown more during that same period of time.

Dawson had plenty of help. The starting running backs, Mike Garrett and Robert Holmes, had speed and power. Warren McVea and Wendell Hayes could spell them with little loss of talent to the team. Wide receiver Otis Taylor was big, fast, and explosive, a gamebreaker. His counterparts, Frank Pitts and Gloster Richardson, were solid. Tight end Fred Arbanas was a devastating blocker and good third-down receiver. The offensive line featured stars like tackle Jim Tyrer, guard Ed Budde, and center E. J. Holub. Mo Moorman and Dave Hill filled out a huge group up front.

Defensively, the Chiefs were possibly the equal

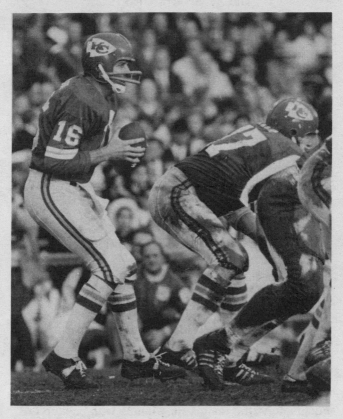

Quarterback Len Dawson overcame injury, the death of his father and having his name linked with a known gambler to lead the Chiefs to their great Super Bowl upset of the Vikings. *(Vernon J. Biever photo)*

of the Vikings. End Jerry Mays and mammoth tackle Buck Buchanan were all-league, while Curley Culp and Aaron Brown were nearly as good. The linebackering corps of Bobby Bell and Jim Lynch on the outside and Willie Lanier in the middle might have been the best trio in all of pro football. Cornerback Emmitt Thomas and safety Johnny Robinson were among the best at their positions. Even the Chiefs' placekicker, Jan Stenerud, was considered better than the Vikes' Fred Cox.

Breaking the game down position by position today, it's hard to see why the Vikings were favored. Maybe it was difficult to shake that old NFL mystique. Kansas City was still considered to be an AFL team, and the AFL was still considered by most to be inferior to the NFL. Part of the reason for the Vikes being heavy favorites could have been the status of Chiefs quarterback Dawson. It had been an extremely difficult year for him, and his problems continued nearly right up to game time.

For openers, Dawson suffered a knee injury against Boston in the second game of the season. That put him on the shelf for the next six games. Fortunately, the team kept winning with backup QB Mike Livingston at the helm. Then, shortly after he returned to action, Dawson had to deal with the death of his father. He came under further criticism when the Chiefs lost their final regular season game to Oakland, 10–6. People openly questioned the game plan.

Then on Tuesday, January 6, just five days before the Super Bowl, another big story broke. It reported a federal investigation into sports gambling and said that Len Dawson was among several pro football players who would be called to testify in Detroit. It could be totally disruptive to a key player so close to game time.

It seems that Dawson's phone number had been found in the possession of a man of dubious reputation who was arrested while carrying $400,000 with him. Dawson admitted he had known the man for about 10 years, but said he had never been associated with him in any business dealings. Dawson prepared a statement for the press stating he had not been contacted by any law enforcement agency regarding the investigation. He also said he had not been told why his name was being brought up except for the telephone number.

"My only conversation with [this man] in recent years concerned my knee injury and the death of my father," Dawson said. "On these occasions he called me to offer his sympathy."

Reaction to the story by Dawson's K.C. teammates was more emotional. In a word, they were angry.

"Lenny is too smart to get mixed up in something like this," said running back Mike Garrett. "To me there's nothing to it, and it doesn't bother me at all."

"We're angry as hell the story came out the way it did," said defensive end Jerry Mays.

Guard Ed Budde spoke for a lot of the Chiefs when he said, "You've got to believe in something, and we believe in Lenny."

Even NFL Commissioner Pete Rozelle issued a statement saying that the league had absolutely no reason to suspect Dawson of any wrongdoing. Any rumors about him were totally unsubstantiated. So after a couple of days the story died down and never surfaced again. But the lingering question was whether this, on top of all the other adversity, would affect Dawson come game time.

The Vikings quarterback, Joe Kapp, was another interesting study. A former All-American at the University of California, Kapp chose to go to the Canadian Football League in spite of his being picked by the Washington Redskins in the 18th round of the 1959 draft. The Vikings had signed him as a free agent in 1967. The Chiefs' Jerry Mays, who had played against Kapp in college, summed up the way the Viking QB could influence the outcome of a game.

"I respect him as much as any guy I've ever played against," Mays explained. "He is a sorry passer and really not a great quarterback, but he's a great leader and real fireball. I hated to play against him.

"You always felt his presence no matter where he was, on the sidelines or on the field. He'd look at you and challenge you with his eyes. When I think of him, I think of his eyes."

When Kapp joined the Vikings in 1967, he quickly showed his new teammates the kind of man he was. After a tough loss to Green Bay, Kapp got into a disagreement with linebacker Lonnie Warwick about the reasons for the defeat. One thing led to another, and pretty soon the two were engaged in a real fist-fight. What came out of it was mutual respect and a new unity among the Vikings.

Kapp had a slogan at the beginning of 1969. It was

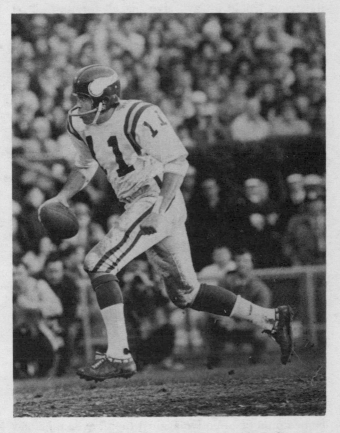

Tough Joe Kapp scrambled for a few short gains in Super Bowl IV, but the Kansas City defense kept the Vikings' quarterback under wraps for most of the afternoon. *(Vernon J. Biever photo)*

"40 for 60" and meant that each of the 40 players on the team would always give his all for the full 60 minutes of the game. It was a rallying cry the whole year. While Kapp was far from a picture passer, he could get the job done. In an early-season game against Baltimore, Joe completed 28 of 43 passes for a then team record of 449 yards. In doing so he also tied an NFL record by throwing seven touchdown passes.

As with most Super Bowls, the focus was on the quarterbacks. This was quite a study in contrasts, the coolly efficient, sometimes unemotional Dawson against the hard-driving, win-any-way-you-can Joe Kapp. But there would be other forces at work, too. For instance, the Vikings were well aware of the Jets' big upset over the Colts the year before. The team knew the entire NFL was looking for them to win, to reestablish the National Football League superiority. K.C., on the other hand, felt their league was just as good as the NFL and wanted to prove it.

Coach Stram also felt there were ways his offense could exploit the rib-rocked Minnesota defense. The Vikings' cornerbacks always played deep and depended on the defensive ends to hurry the quarterback or deflect his passes. Stram felt a short passing game could be effective against them, even if he had to double-team ends Eller and Marshall. Plus his "moving pocket" might also make it work.

Minnesota's Bud Grant just wanted his club to play solid, basic football. He hadn't seen enough of the Chiefs to formulate a specific play. "It's hard to plan for a team when you've only seen them on three films," he said. "All we know about the Chiefs is that their style is similar to that of the Dallas Cowboys."

That, in itself, was a compliment. The Cowboys were one of the finest teams in the NFL. Now it was almost game time. Super Bowl IV would be held at Tulane Stadium in New Orleans, with more than 80,000 fans in attendance. The pressure was mounting. The night before the game Len Dawson awoke with cramps and nausea about 4 A.M. He was up the rest of the night.

Besides pressure, there was also anticipation. The Chiefs' wide receiver Otis Taylor had played in Super Bowl I, when his team was soundly beaten by Green Bay. He felt this was a much improved Kansas City team, and he couldn't wait to prove it.

"We have great new people, unselfish people," Taylor said. "This is the game we've all been waiting for, the pot of gold, ever since we lost that first one."

Finally it was time to play football. There would be no more talking or analyzing until it was over. With the full merger beginning the next season, Super Bowl IV would be the last of its kind. Prestige was on the line for both the teams and the two leagues. In fact, the Chiefs came out wearing a red, white, and blue patch on the shoulder of their uniforms that read "10 AFL." It was a way of honoring the 10 years of American Football League existence.

K.C.'s Jan Stenerud booted the opening kickoff out of the end zone, and the Vikes started the game from their own 20. Staying mainly on the ground,

Minnesota moved the ball to their 35. Then Kapp dropped back for his first pass. He saw double-coverage on the speedy Gene Washington, so he went to tight end John Beasley cutting over the middle. Beasley grabbed the toss in full stride and raced into Kansas City territory to the 39. The Vikings were making it look easy.

But suddenly the K.C. defense toughened. Their big, strong front four and powerful linebackers stopped two running plays. Then another Kapp to Beasley pass fell incomplete. The ball was still at the 39, and Coach Grant opted to punt, rather than try a field goal into the wind. Punter Bob Lee tried to boot the ball out of bounds inside the five, but instead it went out on the 17. Now Dawson and his offense trotted onto the field.

Right away the K.C. offense showed it could move the ball. Three running plays and a pair of completions to Frank Pitts brought the ball into Minnesota territory before the drive stalled. Then Stenerud came on and calmly booted a 48-yard field goal to give Kansas City a 3–0 lead. Then for the rest of the first period the defenses took over. Surprisingly, neither team threatened until the session ended. At this point one thing was sure—the Vikings were not going to roll over the Kansas City Chiefs. Most people still believed they would win, though.

Early in the second period the Chiefs again moved into Viking territory, and Stenerud once again did his thing. This time it was a 32-yard field goal into the wind, and K.C. had a 6–0 lead. It wasn't a big lead, but enough to get the Vikings' attention. They knew their opponents were there to play and play hard.

Midway through the period came a couple of sequences that may have been the turning point. The Vikings were stopped deep in their own territory again when Bob Lee shanked a punt. The ball went out of bounds at the Minnesota 44, and the Chiefs were in business. This time Dawson decided to get tricky. He called an end around and handed the ball to wide receiver Frank Pitts. Pitts skirted the end and raced all the way to the 25 before he was tackled.

K.C. then moved inside the 20 before they were stopped, and Stenerud booted his third field goal of the day. His 25-yarder gave his team a 9–0 lead. Suddenly there were shades of Super Bowl III. Was another major upset in the making? It took only a few minutes to answer that question.

The Vikings' Charlie West was back to field Stenerud's kickoff. He either misjudged the ball or a gust of wind caught it, because it bounced off his body and rolled back upfield. The Chiefs' Remi Prudhomme fell on the ball at the 19, giving Dawson and company another golden opportunity. On the first play from scrimmage, however, the Kansas City QB was sacked for an eight-yard loss.

Like any good quarterback, Dawson noticed that defensive tackle Alan Page was simply charging straight ahead, making him a target for a trap block. On the next play guard Ed Budde executed a perfect block, and Wendell Hayes roared through the hole for a 13-yard gain. Then a short pass to Otis Taylor moved the ball to the five.

The Vikings defense spread out. Dawson knew they were looking for a sweep. He simply faked it by having tackle Jim Tyrer pull out and start toward the sideline. When Page started to go with him, he was again blocked, this time by Mo Moorman. At the same time tight end Fred Arbanas put a crunching block on middle linebacker Lonnie Warwick, and Mike Garrett roared through the created opening into the end zone. Touchdown! Stenerud's extra point made it a 16–0 game, and that's the way the half ended.

It was now apparent that the Chiefs were totally outplaying the Vikings. They had 10 first downs to just four for Minnesota and had 147 total yards to just 95 for the Vikes. Minnesota had crossed midfield just twice but hadn't really threatened either time. The farthest they had penetrated was to the Chiefs' 38. If they didn't make a big halftime adjustment, the Vikings were in trouble. But they had been a great second-half team all year, and there was still confidence in the Minnesota locker room. When the team came back on the field for the second half, they seemed to have newfound fire in their eyes.

The Chiefs controlled the ball for the first six minutes of the third period, again keeping mostly to the ground. Minnesota finally held, and K.C. came away with nothing. Now Kapp was on the field again, exhorting his team to rise to the occasion. For the first time all afternoon the Vikings began moving the ball and dominating the big Kansas City defense.

It took nine plays for them to move from their

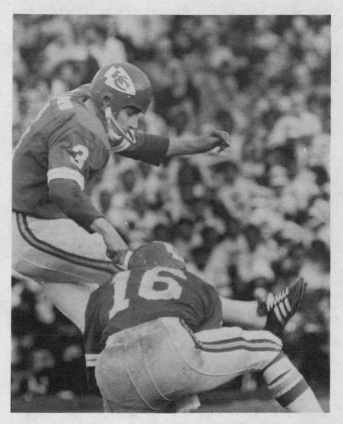

Placekicker Jan Stenerud was one of the first of the soccer-style kickers and one of the best. In Super Bowl IV he booted three field goals, including a 48-yarder that opened the scoring. *(Vernon J. Biever photo)*

own 31 to the K.C. 4. Then halfback Dave Osborn bulled his way over left tackle for the touchdown. Cox's kick cut the margin to 16–7, which, ironically, was the identical score by which the Jets had beaten the Colts the year before. But there was still plenty of time left, and the Vikings had just proved they weren't quitting. They felt they now had the momentum. The Chiefs, however, knew the best way to stop a team with momentum was to take it right back.

So the next possession was a very important one. The Chiefs could only bring the kickoff back to the 18. If the Vikings could force a one-two-three-punt sequence, they could well get the ball back in great field position for another score. Only Kansas City wasn't about to let that happen. Keeping the ball on the ground, Dawson got one first down, then three plays later was facing a third-and-seven on the K.C. 32.

The Viking defenders got ready for another pass, but once again Dawson and the Chiefs fooled them. The heady quarterback called still another end-around, and Frank Pitts carried the ball to the 39, getting a first down by just inches. More important, the drive was still alive and the momentum was beginning to swing back in the direction of Kansas City.

When a roughing-the-passer penalty brought the ball to the Minnesota 46, Viking spirits flagged even more. Dawson hadn't really looked for the big play all afternoon, and he saw no reason to change. He dropped back and threw a sideline pass in the direction of Otis Taylor, who grabbed it for what appeared to be about a 6-yard gain. No one counted, however, on the great talent of Taylor turning the routine into the spectacular.

Cornerback Earsell Mackbee was first on the scene diving at Taylor's legs. He appeared to have the play stopped, but Taylor twisted and turned and somehow broke the tackle. He then began racing down the right sideline where strong safety Karl Kassulke drew a bead on him at the 10. A split second before the collision Taylor made a quick move to the inside, caught Kassulke off balance, and pushed him away with a straight arm. He then charged into the end zone for yet another K.C. score. Stenerud's kick made the score 23–7, and with the fourth quarter almost upon them, it was a commanding lead.

After the game Otis Taylor would remember his outstanding play. "I always try to punish a pass defender just as he does me," Taylor said. "I spun away from the first guy, then hit the last guy down-field with my hand. And I wanted to score that touchdown because I remembered how Minnesota came back to beat the Rams. I felt we needed to continue our scoring."

There was just 1:22 left in the quarter after Tay-lor's TD, but it didn't really matter. The Chiefs were playing with confidence and abandon at this point. They felt it was their game. The offense had done its job, and now it was time for the defense to strut its stuff. They knew Kapp had to throw the football to try to get his team back in the game, and they were ready.

Interceptions by linebacker Lanier and safety Robinson stopped two drives. Then on another, Kapp was hit hard by defensive end Aaron Brown and had to leave the game. Gary Cuozzo replaced him, and when he tried to engineer a drive, he, too, was picked off. The result was inevitable—the Chiefs simply outplayed the Vikings and pulled off a second straight Super Bowl upset. The final score was 23–7. And perhaps just as important was the final tally of the first four Super Bowls. It read NFL 2, AFL 2. Not too many people were arguing against parity now.

Dawson had run the offense flawlessly, completing 12 of his 17 passes for 142 yards and a score. He was named the game's Most Valuable Player, but there were many stars.

"The Kansas City defensive line resembled a redwood forest," said defeated quarterback Joe Kapp. "They took the running game away from us, and we couldn't come up with the big play when we needed it. That's what got us here, but we couldn't do it today. They just played too well defensively."

Minnesota coach Bud Grant also gave the Chiefs their due. Said Grant, "I can't say that Kansas City is the toughest team we've played all year," he said, "but production-wise and point-wise, they outplayed us the toughest."

Quarterback Dawson received a locker room call from President of the United States Richard Nixon. The president congratulated Dawson on a job well done, to which the QB replied, "I didn't do it by myself. Everybody did a great job."

Mr. Nixon also said that he had heard personally from the FBI that there was absolutely no truth in the pregame rumors that Dawson might be connected with gamblers. This also made the quarterback beam. "Mr. President," he said, "I certainly appreciate that because we have always tried to exemplify what is good in professional football."

Dawson also admitted to the press that the allegations had put a great deal of stress on himself and his family, but he said it didn't motivate him to play better.

"I approached this game as a big game, as an opportunity to be the best. You don't need any outside motivation for that."

The following fall the Kansas City Chiefs would be part of the Western Division of the American Football Conference of the National Football League. But on January 11, 1970, the team was still part of the American Football League trying to show the gridiron world they were every bit as good as their National Football League counterparts. Perhaps it was Lamar Hunt, who was not only the owner of the Chiefs but the driving force behind the formation of the AFL, who said it best. Asked to comment on the decade of the AFL that was about to end, Hunt said:

"It's been a lot of fun. I don't even care who started it, but it's nice to know that the Chiefs finished it."

They finished it, all right, in a 23–7 upset that is still talked about today.

Courage Spells Upset

Upsets come in all shapes and sizes. There isn't only one formula that sets the stage for an underdog to rise up and conquer. It sometimes happens when it's least expected. Perhaps the most unusual situation is when the roles flip-flop in midstream. One team enters a playoff series as the odds-on favorite. Yet before it ends, something occurs that completely changes the odds. The favorite becomes the underdog, and an upset is the only way they can win it.

That was exactly what happened to the 1969–70 New York Knickerbockers. They were considered the best team in the National Basketball Association for the entire regular season. The Knicks won 26 of their first 28 games, including a then-record 18 in a row. In doing so, they showed the basketball world that the team concept wasn't dead. Despite the many great individual talents who were in the NBA at the time, the Knicks proved that a carefully balanced team still had the advantage. What would happen, however, to that team when one of its key parts became damaged? That is the real story of the 1969–70 New York Knicks. Let's set the stage.

Many basketball fans looked to the 1969–70 season as one of change. An era had ended the year before when the great center Bill Russell retired from the Boston Celtics. Russell had led the Celts to 11 NBA titles in 13 years, a dynasty-like run that will probably never be duplicated. While the Celts always emphasized strong team play, the ballclub was loaded with individual stars as well. Bob Cousy, Bill Sharman, Tom Heinsohn, Frank Ramsey, John Havlicek, Sam Jones, K. C. Jones, Tom Sanders, and Bailey Howell were all great players in their own right. Russell was the key, however, with his great defense and rebounding. He was the one player the Celts could least afford to lose.

In fact, the late 1950s and 1960s was the era of great centers. Russell's biggest rival was basketball's biggest man, Wilt Chamberlain. Wilt was never surrounded by the same supporting cast as Russell and therefore often finished second best. Other outstanding big men of the decade were Nate Thurmond, Walt Bellamy, Willis Reed, Wes Unseld, and Elvin Hayes.

At the beginning of the 1969–70 season Chamberlain was playing in Los Angeles for the Lakers. When Wilt joined greats Jerry West and Elgin Baylor, many felt L.A. should be favored for the title. Unseld was centering a good Baltimore team. Thurmond was in San Francisco, Hayes in San Diego, and Willis Reed in New York. In addition, the Milwaukee Bucks had a 7-2 rookie out of UCLA named Lew Alcindor. The man who would later change his name to Kareem Abdul-Jabbar was great from his very first day as a pro.

Yet it was the Knicks who set the league on fire almost from the opening game. This was a team that had finished last in its division with a 30-50 record as recently as 1965–66. That was Willis Reed's second year with the club. Reed was a shade under 6'10" and weighed 240 pounds. He wasn't a dominant center like Russell or Chamberlain, but he was a tough and tireless worker at both ends of the floor. Reed averaged 19.5 points a game as a rookie and grabbed 1,175 rebounds. His philosophy was simple.

"In this game," Reed said, "it is survival of the fittest. The strong survive; the weak do not."

Then, prior to the 1965–66 season, the Knicks traded for 6'11" center Walt Bellamy, who had been a sensational rookie with Chicago in 1961. Bellamy's play had become increasingly spotty as the years wore on, and when he joined the Knicks, the emerging Reed had to move to forward. Injuries and some extra weight made the adjustment to forward difficult. It took a year for Willis to adjust, but by 1966–67 he had his scoring average up to 20.9 points a game and grabbed more than 1,000 rebounds once again. The team, however, was just 36–45, still a loser.

In 1967–68 the team was in third place at 43-39. They were beginning to get some more solid players, and midway through the season they had a new coach, William "Red" Holzman. Holzman preached team play and began using a rookie guard, Walt Frazier, with veteran Dick Barnett in the backcourt. Hot-shooting Cazzie Russell was the small forward, while Bill Bradley returned from studies at Oxford in England to play the final 45 games of the season. Bellamy was still the center, with Reed at forward. Some felt this was a situation that had to change.

As one rival NBA coach put it, "If I had a choice, I'd take Reed over any other forward in the league. Then I'd play him at center."

It was in December of 1968, shortly after the start of the new season, that the Knicks made perhaps the most important trade in the history of the franchise. Holzman and team officials finally realized the Bellamy-Reed situation wasn't best for the team. So they sent Bellamy and guard Howard Komives to the Detroit Pistons for a 6'6" forward named Dave DeBusschere. DeBusschere was a 28-year-old veteran who brought scoring, rebounding, and an incredible work ethic to the team. He moved in at the other forward slot and allowed Reed to return to his natural position at center.

The team played amazingly well the rest of the year and finished in third place at 54-28, but only three games behind division-leading Baltimore. In the playoffs the Knicks surprised the Bullets by eliminating them in four games. But then they lost in six to the Celtics in the divisional finals. Still, the team had to be considered a prime contender when 1969–70 rolled around.

With Holzman constantly shouting "See the ball! See the ball!" to his team, the Knicks began to

The trade that brought hardworking forward Dave DeBusschere to the Knicks was the final piece in the championship puzzle. *(Courtesy Basketball Hall of Fame)*

emerge. The coach wanted a complete team that could not only win the game on offense, but could make an impact defensively, too. In fact, in an era where there was more one-on-one ball handling and bigger, stronger players working the ball inside, Holzman was teaching a harassing defense that would disrupt ball handling and restrict big men from moving with the ball. When he screamed, "See the ball!" he wanted to make sure his players were ever alert on defense. If one player went for a steal and missed, another player would be ready to step in to back him up.

In 1969–70 Holzman had a team of smart, heady ballplayers who could exercise his game plan and, in fact, seemed to relish it. Reed, of course, was the center. Willis was a tenacious rebounder and one of the strongest players in the league. His strength helped him handle centers who were inches taller than he was. He could hit his lefty jumper from the outside and score underneath as well. He was not only the team's center, but its enforcer as well. There weren't too many players in the league willing to make Reed angry.

Though he was just 6'6", DeBusschere would be called a power forward today—and he played like one. His sense of position and timing enabled him to outrebound taller, quicker players who were better jumpers. He, too, could hit the long jump shot as well as go to the hoop.

Bill Bradley became the starting small forward, while the explosive Cazzie Russell assumed the role of sixth man, whose job it was to score in bunches off the bench. Bradley was a consummate team player, a deft passer and ball handler who never scored as much as he had at Princeton, though he was still a fine shooter. Dollar Bill, as he was called, understood Holzman's system perfectly, as did all the other players.

Veteran Dick Barnett was at one guard slot. An unorthodox lefty shooter, Barnett was a reliable scorer and underrated defensive player. At 6'4" he was big enough to cover the taller guards and quick enough to stay with the smaller ones. He is the player most often forgotten today when people remember that great Knicks team, but Dick Barnett was an integral part of the ballclub. They couldn't have made it work without him.

At the other guard was Walt "Clyde" Frazier, the man who might be most closely identified with the brand of ball the Knicks played. A first-round pick out of Southern Illinois in 1967, the 6'4" Frazier was a disappointment most of his rookie year. Things began to click the final months of the season, and by the next year he began to emerge as a star.

Clyde was the riverboat gambler on defense, the player who could electrify the Madison Square Garden crowd with his fast hands. While he was also an outstanding passer and a 20-point scorer during his prime years, it was his defense that gave Frazier his identity, and he loved it.

"After I make a steal, I'm really keyed up," Frazier said. "For the next three or four minutes I might just go wild, in spurts. I like to hear the cheers of the crowd. It really psyches me up."

Though Frazier was often the gambler, Bill Bradley explained how the team concept was needed to make Clyde's work pay off. "When Walt gambles and goes for the steal, I have to take his man if he misses," Bradley explained. "If I don't, Walt looks bad, and if that happened often, he would lose confidence that I am there behind him. Eventually he would stop gambling, and our whole defense would fall apart."

The knowledgeable hoop crowds at the Garden understood what was happening and were constantly chanting, *"Defense! Defense! Defense!"* to get their team to come alive. Though the bench wasn't deep, Russell, forward Dave Stallworth, center Nate Bowman, and guard Mike Riorden all made significant contributions to the team effort.

When the season got underway, however, no one really expected the Knicks to come out of the gate the way they did. They won their first six games before losing, and won most of them with relative ease. Then, after the loss, they began to win again, and NBA teams quickly began rethinking their basic strategies. They began to look for new ways to stop the Knicks. A couple of teams tried provoking the Knicks, verbally and with rough play, as well as with actual physical threats. It didn't work. The Knicks kept winning, but Dave DeBusschere showed the results of the rugged NBA play.

"At times my arms are really black and blue," he said. "I usually come out of games against Baltimore scratched somehow because Gus Johnson is quite a physical specimen. Their whole team is physical. Atlanta is that way, too."

After 11 games the Knicks were 10-1. What's more, their defense was holding opponents to 101.3 points a game, best in the league. The team was winning its games by an average margin of 16.1 points. The next best winning margin in the league was held by Milwaukee, and it was only 4.9 points a game. That was how dominating the New Yorkers had been.

The winning streak continued. The team was 16-1

69

and had won 10 straight. You couldn't get much better than that. Besides winning, the team was winning on the road, something that is not always easy in the NBA.

At Milwaukee they won, 109–93, showing the rookie Alcindor the realities of NBA life. At Phoenix the score was 116–99. At San Diego it was 129–111, and at Los Angeles it was 112–102. That one was a bit easier since Wilt Chamberlain was on the shelf recovering from knee surgery. San Francisco fell next, 116–103. The team has just cleaned up the West Coast, as one observer put it.

By the time the winning streak reached 15, it was the talk of the league. That was because the record was 17, set by the Washington Capitols in 1946 and tied by the 1959 Boston Celtics. Could the Knicks top it? They won number 16, then tied the mark with an impressive 138–108 rout of Atlanta. In that game the Knicks exploded in the fourth quarter, outscoring the Hawks by a 38–12 margin. Two nights after that they would be trying for a new record, on the road again, this time in Cincinnati. There was talk of pressure, but Walt Frazier said the way the team was winning kept the pressure off.

"We just didn't have that many nerve-racking games," Clyde said. "We were winning by 20 points a lot of times, and that made it easier than if we were just squeaking by. There might have been more pressure then, but the way we were winning made it no big thing."

A capacity crowd gathered at the Cleveland Arena to see if the Knicks could do it. Though the Royals played out of Cincinnati, some of their home

One of the greatest centers of all time, Wilt Chamberlain recovered from early-season knee surgery to help the Lakers challenge the Knicks for the NBA crown. *(Courtesy Basketball Hall of Fame)*

games were in Cleveland. This was one of them. The Cincy coach was former Celtics great Bob Cousy. Cousy had a good reason for wanting his team to stop the Knicks. He was part of that 1959 Celtics squad that held a share of the record. In addition, the 41-year-old Cousy had activated himself to try to spark some more interest in his team. He hadn't played competitively for seven years.

The game was close all the way. Cincy had a 30–23 lead after one before Cazzie Russell came off the bench in the second quarter to spur the Knicks to a 55–52 halftime advantage. Then in the second half the lead seesawed back and forth. Neither team could pull away. Finally Cincinnati held a 101–98 lead with 1:49 left to play. At that point the Royals' superstar guard, Oscar Robertson, fouled out of the game. In a surprise move Cousy inserted himself in the lineup to replace the Big O.

For the first minute he was in the game, Cousy turned back the clock. First he fired a nifty cross-court hook pass to fellow guard Norm Van Lier, who hit an open jumper. Moments later Cousy himself drew a foul and calmly sank a pair of free throws. With just 26 seconds left, Cousy had sparked the Royals to a 105–100 lead. It looked as if the Knicks' winning streak was about to end.

Great teams have the ability to do great things, though. The Knicks took the ball upcourt quickly, and Barnett hit Reed with a pass underneath. The Knicks captain was fouled trying to put back his own errant shot and made both free throws to bring the score to 105–102. Cincy then called a timeout because Knick pressure wouldn't let them inbound. Now the Royals had the ball at halfcourt.

Cousy tried to pass the ball to Tom Van Arsdale, but DeBusschere beat his rival to the ball, dribbled upcourt, and laid it in. It was now 105–104. All the Royals had to do now was hold the ball and let the clock run out, but the Knicks continued to press. This time Reed deflected the ball to Frazier. Clyde went to the hoop, missed the shot, but was fouled by Van Arsdale. There were just two seconds left.

Calmly the Knick guard made both his charity tosses. Incredibly, the Knicks had taken the lead, 106–105. Cincinnati inbounded, but couldn't get a shot off before the buzzer sounded. The Knicks had done it. They had not only won the game in dramatic fashion, but had set a new NBA record with 18 consecutive victories.

After the game Frazier said, "I was hoping my first shot went in. I didn't want to go to the line having to make the second one for a tie. But as soon as I made the first one, I was confident. If I had missed it, I would have been a little uptight. But when I made the first one, I knew it was over."

The team was now 24-1, an incredible start. They had clearly become the class of the NBA. Then how in the world could anyone call them an underdog? The only way the Knicks could be involved with an upset is if they lost a game. Then their streak ended at 18. While the team would win 26 of its first 28, they began to tail off after that. They were still playing well, but not with the buoyant intensity of those first 25 games.

It's hard to say why a team that was so dominant

abruptly lost some of the magic. Part of the problem was minor injuries. Reed was banged up for a while. Bradley missed about 14 games with a bum ankle. Once the starters slacked off and that fine balance of offense and defense was disrupted, the team lost something. The bench just wasn't that deep.

So after the 26-2 start, the Knicks played 34-20 basketball the rest of the way. They still won the Eastern Division with a 60-22 mark, four games better than the onrushing Bucks, who were being sparked by their great rookie Alcindor. The Knicks still had the best record in the league and, as such, were the preliminary favorites as the playoffs were set to begin.

Most felt the team's biggest threats came from their divisional rivals, Milwaukee and Baltimore. After all, those two clubs had the second and third best records in the league. In the West, Atlanta finished on top with the Lakers next. But there was one other factor when the playoffs began. Wilt Chamberlain had recovered from his early-season knee surgery much faster than anticipated. The big center was healthy and ready to start for the Lakers in the playoffs.

First the Knicks had to deal with the Bullets. The two teams matched up well. Wes Unseld was a strong, tough center, a great rebounder and passer. Earl "The Pearl" Monroe was a great scorer at guard and would someday team with Frazier in the Knicks backcourt. For this series, though, he was the enemy.

The first game at Madison Square Garden set the tone for the series. It was an amazing battle in which neither team would give an inch. The game went into double overtime with the Knicks finally prevailing, 120–117. Again it was defense that spelled the final result. Frazier had four steals in the overtime sessions to help his team win it. Monroe scored 39 points, while Unseld had 31 big rebounds. Reed finished with 30 points and 21 rebounds, while De-Busschere and Bradley had 20 points each. It was that kind of game.

When the Knicks won the second game at Baltimore, they seemed on their way. But the Bullets stormed back and upset the Knicks at the Garden before winning at Baltimore to even the series at two games each. The Knicks took Game Five, 101–80, while the Bullets won the sixth, 96–87. The lower scores indicated how tough and defensive the series was.

Then in the seventh and deciding game, the Knicks once again showed their true mettle. They simply wore the Bullets down and won it, 127–114. The question was how much had the physically brutal series taken out of the Knicks and would they fall prey to the young Bucks and Lew Alcindor in the division finals? They quickly showed they were more than ready.

Once again Coach Holzman used smart team tactics. He had Reed, a strong outside shooter, take young Alcindor away from the basket as much as possible. At the same time Frazier exploited the ball-handling weaknesses of Flynn Robinson, the Bucks' top guard. Robinson didn't like to go left, yet the defensive wizardry of Frazier forced him left for most of the series. As a result, Robinson's offense sputtered.

Thus the Knicks eliminated the Bucks in five games to advance to the NBA championship round. Waiting for them were none other than the Los Angeles Lakers. Once again the series would separate the men from the boys. Walt Frazier talked about the special qualities that were needed to compete in a tension-packed playoff game.

"The guy who comes up with ten baskets in the last quarter of a regular-season game when his team is leading or trailing by 30 points is probably not going to be all that great when the pressure is on," Frazier said. "It's the man who wants to handle the ball in every clutch situation that you really need; the guy who wants to take the key shot or go for the key steal. He's the one who will win a playoff for you."

All five Knick starters had this kind of pressure mentality. They would need it because with Chamberlain back in the middle, the Lakers would be tough. The team had two other all-time greats in the lineup as well. Guard Jerry West and forward Elgin Baylor were both high-scoring performers. Baylor was getting close to the end of the line, but West was still one of the finest clutch performers in the game and had led the league in scoring during the regular season with a 31.2 average.

Because of their great season, the Knicks were still favorites. But Chamberlain made it clear before the first game that he would not be pulled away from the hoop the way Alcindor was.

"If Reed's shooting 20- and 25-footers and if we get beat by them, I'll still let him have them."

In other words Wilt was planning to dominate inside. And at 7'1", 290-pounds, he could do it. The final series began at Madison Square Garden on April 24, 1970. Reed came out of the chute like a man possessed. He scored from the outside, as predicted, but also battled the taller Chamberlain underneath with positive results. By halftime the Reed had scored 25 points, and the Knicks had an 11-point lead.

But some of the fire went out of the New Yorkers after intermission. With Baylor and West leading the way, L.A. wiped out the lead by the end of three. In the fourth the Knicks got a lift from the hot-shooting Cazzie Russell and pulled away for a 124–112 victory. Russell hit eight points during a five-minute stretch in the final session, and Reed finished with 37 points for the night. So the final series seemed to be following the predicted script.

Then in the second game the Lakers showed they wouldn't be pushovers. This one went down to the wire with both teams having a chance to win. It was West who scored the final two points on a pair of clutch free-throws. Next it was Chamberlain who made Riordan alter his last-second drive to the hoop, then blocked Reed's shot in the lane to ensure the win. L.A. won it, 105–103, West scoring 34, and earned a split in New York. Now the series was headed back to Los Angeles.

Game Three was another thriller. The Lakers led in the final minutes, but Dick Barnett got hot and scored nine straight points to bring his team back in it. With the score tied at 100 and the clock ticking down, DeBusschere hit a jumper from behind the foul line to give the Knicks the lead. There were just three seconds left.

Enter Jerry West, miracle worker. The superstar guard took the inbounds pass from Chamberlain, dribbled three times, and launched a prayer some 63 feet from the basket. His momentum on the shot carried him almost to midcourt. Everyone watched as the clock ticked down. *Swish!* It went through and tied the game, just as the buzzer sounded.

"What amazed me," said Knicks sub Bill Hosket, "was that West was concentrating on his follow-through. I was watching him, and he shot the thing like he really figured it was going in."

If there had been a three-point play in the NBA then, the shot would have won the game for L.A. Instead there was a five-minute overtime. West had played all 48 minutes, and in the overtime he was obviously tired. He missed all five shots he took in the extra session, and that helped the Knicks finally take a 111–108 victory and a 2-1 lead in the series.

Game Four also went into OT. If the Knicks won, they would return to New York with a commanding 3-1 lead. But the Lakers fought them off and tied the series with a 121–115 triumph. West had 37 points and 18 assists, Baylor scored 30, and Wilt grabbed 25 rebounds. The L.A. big three had really made their presence felt in this one.

Now it was back to the Garden and the crucial fifth game, a game that will be remembered by New York Knicks fans forever. For it was the game that spawned a legend. It happened late in the first quarter. Willis Reed, who had been averaging 25.9 points in 16 playoff games, was operating on progressively tender knees. But the big guy continued to pump up and down the floor.

With 3:56 left in the quarter and the Knicks leading, 25–15, Willis had the ball and tried to drive past Chamberlain. Suddenly the big guy lost his footing and fell hard to the floor, landing on his right side. He wasn't getting up. And when he was finally helped to his feet, it was apparent that the Knicks' captain couldn't put much weight on his right leg.

While Reed was being examined in the locker room, the Lakers began taking advantage of Reed's absence. They caught the Knicks, passed them, and led 53–40 at the half. That was when the Knicks learned that Reed had two severely strained muscles in his right thigh. He was through for the night and possibly for the remainder of the series. It was at that precise moment that the odds changed. With Reed out and with the likes of West, Baylor, and Chamberlain on the court for the Lakers, how could L.A. possibly lose? After all, once Reed went down, the Lakers quickly erased a 10-point deficit and rode it to a 13-point halftime lead. That was a 23-point turnaround, 38–15, in little more than 15 minutes.

Meanwhile, the Knicks discussed some Reed-less strategy. They decided to go into a 1-3-1 offense, using DeBusschere as a "rover" down low and forcing Chamberlain to play him. Frazier would control the ball, while Barnett, Bradley, and Russell alternated between the wings and a high pivot. Defensively the team would double-team, harass, gamble, and press.

It was apparent immediately that the Knick strategy was working. The Lakers suddenly seemed out of synch, unable to adjust to the frenetic Knickerbocker play. By the end of the third quarter the lead had melted to 82–75. In the fourth the Knicks kept coming, even when Dave Stallworth had to replace DeBusschere, who sat with five fouls.

The Knicks finally tied it at 87–87, and a Bradley jumper with 5:19 left gave the New Yorkers the lead at 93–91. From there the Knicks continued to press and gamble and shoot well. They surprised everyone—the Lakers, their own fans, and maybe even themselves—winning the game by a 107–100 score. It gave them a 3-2 lead in the series. But how much farther could they go without their leader and pivotman?

As for the Lakers, Coach Joe Mullaney admitted his team wasn't ready for the way the Knicks came out for the second half. "We've been playing a certain style of game," he said. "All these playoff games have been nearly the same. Then they sped it up like a fast movie, switched it around 100 percent."

Now it was back to L.A. for Game Six. Willis Reed stayed behind in New York for treatment on his leg. Meanwhile, Coach Holzman abandoned the emergency strategy of Game Five and went back to a more conventional game plan with 6'10" Nate Bowman starting in Reed's place. It didn't work. Chamberlain exploded for 45 points, and the Knicks seemed listless. The final was 135–113, evening the series once more. With Reed still highly doubtful for the seventh game and a part-time player at best, the Lakers were now the heavy favorites. The roles had reversed completely.

It's hard to describe how much the Knicks missed a player like Willis Reed. There was his obvious talent, of course. There was also more. One NBA veteran told of an encounter he once had with Reed. He was far from the only player who felt this way.

"I once hit Willis in the mouth with my elbow as I came down with a rebound," the player said, "and I apologized fast, as fast as I could get it out of my mouth. I remembered almost hooking up with Willis earlier in the year, and he said to me then, 'I own this court when I'm out here. I'm the king bee.' And I knew he meant it."

There was no announcement by the Knicks before the start of Game Seven whether Reed would play or not. A capacity Garden crowd of 19,500 fans buzzed in anticipation. Even when the Knicks came out to warm up, there was no sign of the captain. Maybe Reed just couldn't make it. Then, shortly before the tip-off, there was Reed, making his way from the locker room to the court surrounded by a cordon of security guards. He seemed to be moving gingerly on his right leg.

When his familiar visage appeared, however, a huge roar went up from the huge crowd. It was the kind of roar that sends shivers up your spine. Even the Lakers stopped warming up momentarily to watch Reed come onto the court. When the starting lineups were announced, Reed was among them. He would play. But how well?

The first time the Knicks had the ball, Reed trailed the action. It was apparent he couldn't move

When he was on the basketball court, Willis Reed felt he was the king bee. But it was the courage the Knicks' center showed after he was hurt that inspired his teammates to their greatest victory. *(Courtesy Basketball Hall of Fame)*

very well. He was not close to being at full strength. The Lakers should have been able to take advantage of this, but as Willis limped into the offensive end, the ball was kicked out to him and he took a quick jumper. It went in and the crowd erupted.

Minutes later he hit his second shot, and again the energy flowed through the Garden. Still, it was obvious that the captain was laboring. He tried to lean on Chamberlain defensively, but the leg was getting weaker. Yet over the next several minutes the Knicks went on a roll. Once again their defense was paying off. The Lakers were making mistakes, and the Knicks were converting, running the score to 17–8.

Reed couldn't hang on much longer. He wouldn't score another point after those first two jumpers, but his tremendous courage had inspired his teammates. For the remainder of the first half (though Reed had gone to the bench) the Knicks played as if no force on earth could beat them. With Walt Frazier leading the way, New York raced to a 69–42 halftime lead, an incredible feat considering Reed wasn't Reed and then looking at the caliber of talent on the Los Angeles side of the court.

In the second half the Lakers closed the gap, but it was so huge the Knicks just hung on, continuing to play their special kind of team basketball. The fans enjoyed the countdown as the final minutes ticked away. Then it was over. The New York Knicks had won it, 113–99, and were champions. Frazier led the way with 36 points and a record-tying 19 assists. DeBusschere had 18 points and 17 rebounds. Barnett chipped in with 21 and Bradley with 17. Team play, once again.

Knick fans have looked back upon the 1969–70 season many times since then. It's a memory to savor. Reed would have an injury-plagued career after that, but he was healthy enough to help his club to another title three years later. But the first, to most, was the best.

That was because the Knicks went into the play-offs as the favorites. They were supposed to win. After the big guy was hurt, they were no longer the favorites. Then they weren't supposed to win. But with a big dose of courage, and an incredible amount of team play, the Knicks wound up pulling off a great upset, defeating a team that had three of the best players of all time. That's the stuff dreams—and upsets—are made of.

The Longest Jump

There's an old axiom in sports that says records are made to be broken. It has been proved true in almost all cases. Even those records that have stood the test of time are still vulnerable because the athletes keep coming. Training methods improve. Equipment gets better. The will to exceed one's own limits remains strong. Thus—records are made to be broken.

In some ways, individual records are more intriguing than team marks. To watch an athlete work toward breaking a mark over and over again, and finally doing it, is always inspiring. Sometimes the athlete expected to set a new standard doesn't do it. Instead, another athlete, an underdog, puts forth a singular incredible effort and surprises everyone. This is another form of a great upset.

Some individual records have proved much more

difficult to break than others. Swimming records, for instance, seem to change nearly every year. In track and field, some records (pole vault, decathlon) seem to topple almost with regularity. Others are more difficult to crack.

One of those has always been the long jump. Even its name has changed. Years ago the event was known as the broad jump. But one fact remains constant. In some 56 years between 1935 and 1991, only four different athletes held the long jump record. The first held it for 25 years, and the fourth had it all to himself for 23 years. When the record was finally broken again, it ranked as one of the biggest upsets in years.

The story begins back in 1935, and it begins with a legend. His name was Jesse Owens, a man who, to this day, is still considered by many the greatest track and field performer America has ever produced. Owens performed in an era when training methods, equipment, and even nutritional knowledge weren't nearly so advanced as they are today. Yet he was still brilliant.

Owens was just a 21-year-old sophomore at Ohio State University when he produced what is still considered the finest one-day showing in track history. In one afternoon Jesse Owens set three world records and tied another while competing in four different events. First he tied the record for the 100-yard dash (9.4 seconds). He then set new marks in the 220-yard dash (20.3 seconds), the 220-yard low hurdles (22.6 seconds), and finally in the long jump. In that event Owens leapt 26 feet, 8¼ inches.

A year later Owens made Olympic history. Competing in Berlin, Germany, in 1936, the American star won four gold medals, winning the 100- and 200-meter dashes and the long jump, plus helping the United States 4 × 100–meter relay team to a victory. And he did it under pressure. Germany, at the time, was under the yoke of Adolf Hitler, who had proclaimed before the Games began that his Aryan athletes were superior to America's "black auxiliaries."

Owens's track records would fall one by one. But the mark that lasted the longest was his 26′ 8¼″ long jump. It would be a full quarter century before another athlete would jump farther than Jesse Owens did in 1935. Finally, in 1960, the record fell—to another American, Ralph Boston.

For the next eight years Boston and Russian jumper Igor Ter-Ovanesyan were the best in the world. They dueled on an international stage, and their great rivalry slowly inched the record upward. Each broke the other's mark several times. Finally, when it was time for the 1968 Olympics, Ter-Ovanesyan held the mark at 27′ 4¾″. So in 33 years the record had only been extended by 8½ inches.

Boston and Ter-Ovanesyan were expected to battle once again for the gold medal. The '68 Games were being held in Mexico City. Because the city is located well above sea level, the air is thin and thus has less resistance to a moving mass. Some felt there was a good possibility of another new mark in the long jump. Would it be Boston or Ter-Ovanesyan? They were the two expected to do it.

What happened in Mexico City, however, has never been forgotten. It was not either of the two favorites who grabbed the spotlight, but rather an unheralded jumper named Bob Beamon. Beamon was a 22-year-old and certainly a world-class jumper—you have to be world class to make the Olympics—but he wasn't considered a threat for the gold. Most people figured a bronze medal (third place) was a realistic goal for him.

Then came THE JUMP! With the two favorites in the competition dueling for the gold, Beamon got ready for another of his jumps. He thundered down the runway, arms pumping, hit the takeoff board, and was airborne. Suddenly Bob Beamon was flying as no man had flown before. He hung in the air, pumped his arms and legs, then landed near the far end of the pit. Though he knew he had gotten off a good jump, neither Beamon, his competitors, nor anyone else who saw it realized what had happened.

When the tape came out, the officials had to look twice, then a third time. Bob Beamon had obliterated the world record in the long jump by leaping 29' 2½". It was a jump thought impossible by human standards. Remember, the old record was 27' 4¾". Beamon became not only the first man to jump more than 28 feet, but also the first to go past 29 feet. He had beaten the old mark by some 21¾ inches.

Ter-Ovanesyan, who was slated to jump next, hesitated. "I was ashamed to jump," he said later. "Bob had left us and gone on to a new world."

When Beamon learned what he had done, he collapsed on the field and cried. That's how astonishing his leap had been. Some said, flat out, it was a mark that would never be broken. It was hailed as the greatest single feat in track and field history. Because he had beaten not only the best, but the odds as well, Beamon's jump was in itself a great upset.

It was apparent that the high altitude of Mexico City helped. Scientific estimates said he might have gained almost 8 inches because of the altitude. If that was the case, he still would have broken the record by more than a foot. There was no way to discredit the mark. It belonged to Bob Beamon.

Even Beamon was overwhelmed. He never again jumped even 27 feet in competition. Perhaps he knew he could never approach the record again. The question was, could anyone else? The answer was a decided no—that is, until Carl Lewis came along.

A native of Birmingham, Alabama, Lewis burst on the track scene as a 19-year-old in 1981. Because of his versatility, he was compared with Jesse Owens right from the beginning. A sprinter and a long jumper, Lewis won the Sullivan Award as the nation's finest amateur athlete in '81.

In February of that year, Lewis was beaten in a long jump competition by Larry Myricks. It would be the last time anyone would defeat him in that event for an entire decade. Coached by Tom Tellez at the University of Houston, Lewis began using his sprinter's speed and athletic ability to perfect his skills as a long jumper. Before long people were saying that if anyone had a chance to break Bob Beamon's record, it was Carl Lewis.

Then in the 1984 Olympics at Los Angeles, Lewis captured the headlines by duplicating Jesse Owens's quadruple gold-medal performance of nearly half a century before. Lewis won gold in the 100- and 200-meter dashes, the long jump, and in the 4×100–

The great Carl Lewis strains for every extra inch during his gold medal–winning performance in the long jump at the summer Olympics in Barcelona, Spain, in 1992. Lewis won the gold by beating archrival and world-record holder Mike Powell. *(AP/Wide World Photo)*

meter relay. Lewis was being hailed as one of the greatest all-around performers ever in his sport.

But he was far from through. He continued to win accolades and track meets, and he began pursuing Bob Beamon's long jump record in earnest, putting together a string of jumps in the 28-foot range. He won more gold at the Olympics in '88, including another triumph in the long jump. Coming in to the 1991 season, Lewis had not been beaten in the long jump for nearly 10 years. He had totally dominated the event.

In September of 1991, Lewis joined many of the world's best track and field athletes for the highlight meet of the season, the World Track and Field Championships held in Tokyo, Japan. Though he was now 30 years old, the competitive fires still burned, and Lewis pointed toward a pair of glamour events, the 100-meter dash and the long jump. He wouldn't mind breaking world records in both events.

Most experts felt that the 100-meter dash would be difficult. After all, Lewis would be running against world record holder Leroy Burrell and a select group of elite sprinters. But in the long jump, well, that event had simply been Lewis's domain for so long that people often didn't think twice about it. Carl would jump and Carl would win. The only question was how far would he go?

There was one man, however, who did stand a chance against Lewis in the long jump. His name was Mike Powell, and he had been chasing number one for a long time. Powell, 27, was three years younger than Lewis and had been the silver medalist behind Lewis in the 1988 Olympics. Though he had never beaten Lewis in 15 tries, he had come close. Just a few months earlier at a national meet in June, Lewis needed his final jump to beat Powell by a scant half inch.

Powell had leapt 28′ 3¾″ that day, and over the years he had fouled on longer jumps. He never stopped believing that he had some very big jumps deep within him, and he kept working hard to bring them out.

"Carl is a sprinter who jumps," said Randy Huntington, Powell's coach. "Mike is a *jumper*. His speed in the last 10 meters before the board is almost as great as Carl's."

Powell's biggest struggle was to get his approach and overall technique under control. He often had problems with his mechanics, and that was one reason for the high number of fouls. Though he won silver at the Seoul Olympics in '88, he wasn't close to topping Lewis. Yet when his coach met longtime record-holder Beamon, Randy Huntington introduced himself in a very confident way.

"I'm the guy who's going to coach the guy who's going to break your record," he said.

Mike Powell was born in Philadelphia and moved to California when he was 11. At Edgewood High in West Covina, California, the 6′1″, 150-pound Powell was quite an athlete. On the basketball court he would often dunk the ball over opposing centers. On the track he was already a 7-foot high jumper. Yet he was strangely neglected by the colleges, and it upset him. Maybe so much that his drive to excel was sharpened.

"People I had beaten were getting better scholarship offers than I was," Powell said. "It was hard for me to understand, because I had a 3.2 grade point average, scored over 1,000 on my SATs, and was an academic All-American."

Finally he went to the University of California at Irvine, where he gave up basketball to concentrate on track. When he long jumped 26' 5¼" as a sophomore, he decided to concentrate on that event. It wasn't long after that that he began chasing Lewis. Coming into Tokyo, Powell had worked himself up to a 28' 7¾" jumper, certainly within reach of 29 feet and maybe a record.

His main battle was to get his emotions under control. Sometimes he was so pumped up that it led to fouls. Some other jumpers on the circuit even called him "Mike Foul," not a flattering nickname for a world-class jumper. Coach Randy Huntington said, "Mike is an emotional jumper. His technique often depends on the height of his emotions."

In other words, Powell had to relax and compete. After coming so close to Lewis at the June nationals, he seemed to get an extra shot of confidence.

"After that I told a lot of people I was going to get him the next time we met," Powell said.

They were supposed to clash at a meet in August, but Lewis suddenly withdrew, saying his back was bothering him in the cold, damp weather. It just made Powell more determined and created a degree of animosity between the two.

"He ran from me at Sestierre [the site of the meet]," said Powell. "If you're going to be a champion, you have to be a champion under all conditions, not just when everything is going your way."

Two of Powell's foul jumps at that meet measured more than 29 feet. He seemed to be coming into Tokyo as the hot jumper. But whenever there was a long jump competition, Lewis was the heavy favorite. Then, early in the championships, it was Carl Lewis writing the story.

Not only did Lewis defeat Leroy Burrell and win the 100-meter dash, he also broke the world record with a 9.86 clocking, a feat made more amazing by Lewis's age. At 30 he was considered an old man in an event traditionally dominated by much younger runners. Once again he was hailed as a living legend of the track—which he was. Now, if he could break the long jump record in the same meet, people would probably be calling him the greatest ever in his sport.

Finally it was time for the long jump. As Powell got ready for his first jump in the finals, he was struck by an old foe, his emotions. He was hyperventilating so badly that he jumped just 25' 9¼", not even a world-class leap.

"I was so hyped up to beat Carl that I couldn't even breathe," Powell said.

So as Lewis prepared for his first leap, Powell tried to stay cool, telling himself to calm down, that there was no need to be so psyched up, that he should relax and simply let his ability take over and do the work. Then Lewis came down the runway and jumped 28' 5¾", already a meet record and possibly good enough to win the competition. So the pressure was squarely on Mike Powell.

Relaxed now, Powell shortened his steps and jumped a controlled 28' ¼". It was still well short of

Lewis's first leap, but at least he was over 28 feet and hadn't fouled. Then Lewis served the first notice that this was not going to be an ordinary competition. On his third leap he really soared, landing in the pit 28' 11¾". Though he was wind-aided, it was the longest jump of his life. Wind-aided jumps count in the competition, but do not count as world records.

Powell then took a step backward. His third jump produced a 27' 2½" mark, not good at all. Then Lewis flew down the runway again and leapt. He soared once more. This one felt special. The distance was 29' 2¾". It was ¼ inch over the record, but the wind reading was again over the limit. Lewis had done it, but it wouldn't count as a new mark. He threw his arms up, but at the same time looked confident. He felt he could do it again.

Many athletes in Powell's shoes would have been totally discouraged by now. He had three jumps left, and Lewis had already jumped a foot farther than he had. He gave it a little extra on his fourth jump, but fouled. Now there were two jumps left.

As he got ready for his fifth jump, Mike Powell began to feel it was now or never. Lewis was putting together a great series. He might be able to go even farther. Powell still hadn't broken a big one. He had to do it now.

Like most long jumpers, he stood on the runway in deep concentration. It was almost as if he was meditating, seeing a huge jump in his mind. Then he took four long walking steps, swinging his arms loosely. From there he broke into his run, gathering speed and bringing his knees up higher and higher.

He didn't want to foul and hit the board with nearly two inches to spare. As was his style, Powell drove hard off his left leg and propelled his body upward and outward.

In the air he did a hitch kick for more distance, then threw his legs out in front of him for the landing. As soon as he hit the pit, he knew he had gotten off a big jump. He swung his body to the right and ran out of the pit. He hadn't fouled, the wind reading was faint. It was a legal jump. He paced nervously as the judges measured the jump. It must have seemed like an eternity. The announcement brought a roar from the huge crowd.

Mike Powell had jumped 29′ 4½″. He had broken Bob Beamon's world record! He had done what was considered almost impossible for all jumpers with the exception of Carl Lewis. Powell jumped up and down, spinning and dancing. But he still couldn't go wild in celebration. Lewis had two more jumps.

"I still thought he would beat me," Powell admitted later. "Deep down inside I thought he would do nine meters [29′ 6½″]."

For a split second after the measurement Lewis looked almost shocked. Then he almost seemed to smile, and he began preparing for his fifth jump. He was a pressure performer. Maybe this was just what he needed to push himself over the top. Lewis again sprinted down the runway, hit the board, and soared. The crowd erupted again. Once more Carl Lewis had hit a big one. The measurement was 29′ 1¼″. This time it was against a slight wind. It was the longest legal jump of his life, but still short of Powell's best.

Just minutes after his record-breaking leap of 29 feet, 4½ inches in Tokyo, Mike Powell sits in silent prayer as he watches Carl Lewis prepare for his final jump. *(AP/Wide World Photo)*

One more time Lewis prepared. This time Powell folded his hands as if in prayer as his rival thundered down the approach. There was a sharp bang as Lewis's foot hit the board, and he was airborne once again. This time he jumped 29 feet even, another great leap, but Mike Powell had won. He had not only upset Carl Lewis, handing him his first long jump defeat in a decade, but he had upset even greater odds, breaking a 23-year-old record that people thought only Lewis might break.

Now Powell really celebrated. He hugged a board judge, saying, "I wanted to hug somebody. He was in the way, so he got a hug." Then he hugged his coach, Randy Huntington, telling him, "We got it and we got him," meaning Lewis.

Powell's great upset and record-breaking performance made news all over the world. While his great feat couldn't be denied, there was a little tarnish on the gold ring. Most reporters also wrote of Lewis's great series of jumps. While Mike Powell had one super leap, Carl Lewis had made the four longest jumps of his life. Lewis had mentioned this as well, adding, "Mike had one great jump. He may never do it again. I could have gone farther on my last jump, but I didn't. That's something I have to accept."

The remarks caused a mild controversy. Powell was upset for a while. "For him not to really acknowledge what I did kind of made me upset, but I understand," he said. "After a while, he'll be at peace with it, maybe."

Later Lewis finally did acknowledge his rival's leap. "It was the greatest meet I ever had," he said, referring to his world record in the 100 in addition to his long jump series. "Mike had incredible form. He jumped a world record. He deserved it."

It took 23 years for Bob Beamon's record to fall. Just because Mike Powell now has the mark, Carl Lewis isn't about to quit. He knows how close he came, and he knows that he, too, can go even farther. In August of 1992 it was Lewis who won the Olympic gold medal at Barcelona, Spain, jumping 28' 5½". Powell had trouble with his technique and took the silver medal with a jump of 28′ 4¼″ on his final try. No world record for either man, but another Lewis triumph.

So Mike Powell must be ready to accept more challenges. Despite his second-place finish at Barcelona he is now operating with renewed confidence. His world record and great upset at the World Championships have told him the kind of jumper he can be.

"I've had even longer fouls," he joked. "Now I know I can do 29 feet, not consistently, but legally. I'm a different jumper now. Let's say I've stepped into a different realm."

The biggest goal for Mike Powell in upcoming years is to stay there.

Out with the Old,
In with the New

For six years the Chicago Bulls knew they had the best player in basketball, but could they ever be the best team? Some critics said no. They said that Michael Jordan was so immensely talented as an individual that the Bulls would always suffer as a team. So for both the Bulls and for Michael Jordan, there was something to prove. It wouldn't come easy, not the way it started out.

Chicago picked Michael Jordan on the first round of the 1984 collegiate draft. He was the third player taken. Houston had picked first and tabbed center Akeem Olajuwon of the University of Houston. That was no surprise. Olajuwon was the best center in college ball, a certain future impact player as a pro. The surprise came next. With a chance to pick

Jordan, the Portland Trail Blazers instead chose 7-foot center Sam Bowie of Kentucky. Bowie was coming off two straight injury-plagued seasons, and his future was doubtful. Portland had decided to gamble.

The Bulls couldn't believe Jordan was still available, and they chose him without a moment's hesitation. They were getting a 6'6" guard who was coming out of the University of North Carolina after his junior year and three incredible seasons. As a freshman starter, it was Jordan's clutch jump shot with 15 seconds left that had won a national championship for the Tar Heels. The next two seasons Jordan was college basketball's Player of the Year.

Working under coach Dean Smith's team-oriented system, Michael Jordan compiled good, but not spectacular statistics. More important, he learned to become a team player and to appreciate the total team game. These were qualities that would eventually become invaluable to his own performance and to his teams as well. Though Michael Jordan would reap a slew of individual honors and awards, he wasn't satisfied. Like all very great players, his top priority was his team. The Chicago Bulls had to become not only winners, but champions.

It would be a long road. In the two years before Michael joined the team, the Bulls had records of 28-54 and 27-55. They weren't even close to making the playoffs. Obviously, there was a lack of talent. Michael's first contract called for $3.75 million spread over five years. As it turned out, the contract was a bargain.

Former NBA guard Kevin Loughery was the Bulls'

coach in 1984–85. As soon as he saw the kind of talent Michael had, he turned him loose, allowing him to be creative and freelance on the court. There would be no restraints as there had been at North Carolina. Almost from day one, Michael Jordan became the NBA's most spectacular offensive player. There were nights when he seemed to score almost at will. His leaping ability was incredible, and he had the uncanny talent to hang in the air—almost suspend himself—while making three or four moves to shake his defenders.

By the middle of his rookie season, Michael was battling for the league lead in scoring with Bernard King of the Knicks. And he was leading the Bulls in almost everything—scoring, rebounding, assists, steals, and minutes played. He was an alternate on the Eastern Division All-Star squad and had his team playing close to .500 ball at 20-21. He was the most talked about player to enter the NBA since Magic Johnson and Larry Bird had come in some five years earlier.

Fans all over the league looked forward to seeing the spectacular rookie. As Phoenix Suns' marketing director Harvey Shank put it, "Michael Jordan is already in a class by himself. It's the way he gives himself to the game and his God-given talents. Michael Jordan coming to town is like a major entertainer appearing in Phoenix."

During the season Michael signed a contract with Nike and the "Air Jordan" basketball shoe was born. It would revolutionize the shoe business and become a huge seller with Michael as its articulate

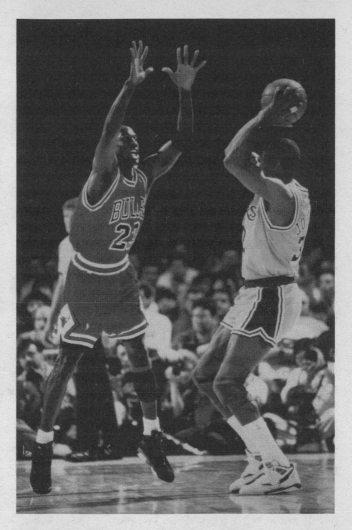

When the Bulls met the Lakers for the NBA title, basketball fans the world over relished the meeting of NBA greats Michael Jordan and Magic Johnson. Here Magic tries to get off a shot as defender Jordan looks to stop him. *(John W. McDonough photo)*

spokesman. He was the perfect new-age athlete. His agent, David Falk, explained why.

"In the age of TV sports," Falk said, "if you were to create a media athlete and star for the nineties—spectacular talent, midsize, well-spoken, attractive, accessible, old-time values, wholesome, clean, natural, not too goody two-shoes, with a little bit of deviltry in him—you'd invent Michael."

During the second half of the season, Michael continued on a roll. He led his team in scoring for 17 straight games at one point, and during that time had games of 42, 36, 35, 38, 45, 38, 41, and 49 points. No one player could stop him. The Lakers' Michael Cooper was about the same size as Jordan and one of the best defensive players in the NBA. Yet Cooper knew the effect Jordan had on even the best defenders.

"There's no way I can stop him," Cooper said flat out. "I need the whole team. As soon as he touches the ball, he electrifies the intensity inside you. The alarm goes off because you don't know what he's going to do. He goes right, left, over you, around and under you. He twists, he turns. And you *know* he's going to get the shot off. You just don't know when and how. That's the most devastating thing psychologically to a defender."

Michael averaged 28.2 points a game as a rookie. King averaged more, but Jordan scored the most points since King missed the last part of the season because of an injury. A broken foot early in his second season kept Michael on the shelf most of 1985–86. But since that time he has been the NBA's scoring champion every year right through 1991–92.

He's also won every individual award possible. Almost every game he plays is a highlight film by itself. But what about the Bulls during this period?

The team finished 38-44 Michael's rookie year and made the playoffs. But they were beaten in the first round. A year later, with Michael injured, they were just 30-52. Still, they sneaked into the playoffs and were beaten three straight by the Celtics. Michael returned for the playoffs, and in the second game, a double-overtime thriller that the Celtics won, Michael Jordan scored an amazing 63 points. He was back.

In 1986–87 Michael won his first NBA scoring title by averaging 37.1 points a game. He became the first player since Wilt Chamberlain to score more than 3,000 points in a season and the first ever to have more than 200 steals (236) and 100 blocks (125) in the same season. The Bulls finished at 40-42 and were again swept by the Celtics in the first round of the playoffs.

Though he was winning more and more individual honors and becoming one of the most recognizable athletes in the world, Michael wasn't satisfied. He wanted his team to win. In fact, one day he stormed off the court because Coach Doug Collins lost track of the score during a scrimmage.

"I'm a competitor and I want to win," Michael said later. "I always keep score in everything—scrimmages, games, whatever—and I know the score was 4-4. Doug said it was 4-3, my team losing. . . . People may think this is all trivial, but when you're a competitor and want to win, nothing is trivial."

In 1987–88 the Bulls drafted a pair of rookie forwards, 6'10" Horace Grant and 6'7" Scottie Pippen. They were both players with considerable natural talent. Steady John Paxson was the other starting guard alongside Michael, and Dave Corzine was the center. Power forward Charles Oakley was another tough inside player. The team, however, wasn't expected to be a whole lot better, but they were. In fact, they were the surprise team of the NBA, winning 12 of their first 15 games out of the gate.

With Michael putting together his greatest all-around season, the Bulls finished at 50-32, good enough for second place in their division. Michael would be the league's Most Valuable Player for the first time and was also named Defensive Player of the Year. No one player had ever won both those prizes at the same time.

In the playoffs the Bulls advanced past the Cleveland Cavaliers, 3-2, but then were beaten in five games by the always tough Detroit Pistons. They were getting closer, but not close enough. Before 1988–89 the team made a big trade with the New York Knicks, getting veteran 7'1" center Bill Cartwright in return for power forward Oakley. Young Horace Grant would move in at the power forward slot.

The team needed a period of adjustment to get its new players into the flow. Then Pippen missed part of the year with back surgery. Michael won another scoring title, but the club finished at 47-35, in fifth place. If they were going to make a move in the playoffs, it would have to be a team effort. Bulls general manager Jerry Krause had even remarked that the team sometimes depended on Michael too much. He was so good that the other players would often stand around, figuring Jordan would get the job done.

But in the playoffs of 1988–89 it began changing. First the Bulls defeated the Cavaliers, 3-2. Jordan made the winning shot in the fifth and deciding game. Next came the New York Knicks. Jordan led the way, as usual, but the other players were all contributing. The result was the Bulls took the series in six. Jordan canned two free throws in the closing seconds of the sixth game to put it away.

Next came the Detroit Pistons. The future champs beat the Bulls in six rough games to win the Eastern Conference title and advance to the championship round. However, the Bulls had come close. Maybe now the team would be looked upon as winners, not just a ballclub that featured basketball's greatest player.

It was more of the same in 1989–90. Jordan had another banner year. Pippen was becoming a star in his own right, a player much like Jordan in many ways. Grant was en route to becoming a force on the inside, while the bench was stronger with center Will Purdue, center-forward Stacey King, and guard B. J. Armstrong. In addition, the team had a new coach in former NBA player Phil Jackson.

The team had a 55-27 season, second only to the Pistons in the Central Division. Jordan was still Jordan. He had 21 games of 40 or more points and a career best of 69 in an overtime win against Cleveland. It was the other players, however, who were getting better. The Bulls were finally becoming a real solid basketball team.

In the playoffs the team won its first two series, then had a return engagement with the Pistons for the Eastern Conference title. Detroit won the first two, its defense again dominating the Bulls. There were stories that Michael Jordan had become angry with the play of his teammates and told one reporter, "If my teammates think I'm going to carry them again, they're wrong!"

What Jordan said to the other Bulls may never be known. But Horace Grant admitted that the superstar gave the other guys a wake-up call.

"He said the guys were playing lousy ball," said Grant. "He didn't want to name names, but he was right. The guys knew who they were. We were embarrassed. Mike felt the guys weren't giving their all, and I don't blame him. We played terribly, and I've never seen Michael that upset."

Even Coach Jackson didn't mind his star venting his feelings to the rest of the team. "When the captain demands something out of his club, it is his prerogative," Jackson said. "He has the right. If we can't take a little adversity, we are not in the hunt the right way."

In Game Three Jordan again led by example. He scored 47 points, 31 of them in the second half and 18 in the final quarter. Pippen also played inspired ball with 29, and the Bulls won, 107–102. They were back in it. Horace Grant, who had 10 points and 11 rebounds, gave credit to the team's superstar.

"I think Michael has given us confidence," Grant said.

The Bulls also won the fourth game, but back in Detroit for Game Five, the Pistons defense prevailed, 97–83. This time Chicago wouldn't quit. They won Game Six 109–91 and were one win away from going to the NBA finals. The final game turned into a disaster. Pippen had a bad migraine headache and was ineffective. Guard John Paxson had to sit out with an ankle sprain. The Pistons won it, 93–74, but the Bulls still felt they were coming together as a team.

"Michael knows he didn't carry us," said Pippen. In the eyes of many the Bulls had paid their dues. Sometimes it takes a young and emerging team several years to get over that playoff hump. Playoff basketball in the NBA is often intense, very physical, and with an emphasis on defense. Teams need that valuable experience to learn to cope. Now the Bulls were in the conference finals twice. They came within one game against the Pistons in 1989–90. No more knocking on the door. If they were ever going to kick it in, it should be in 1990–91.

There was no doubt that the Bulls were a more confident and experienced team. Jordan was still the top scorer in the league, but as the team became better, his scoring average was down slightly. There was never any question about Jordan's willingness to play a team game. He had done that at North Carolina. Put a championship team around him, and he would do anything necessary to win.

Chicago was one of the top NBA teams throughout the season, often winning with ease, yet also showing the ability to dig down deep and come out winners in the close ones. When the regular season ended, the team had won the Central Division title with a franchise best record of 61-21. They finished 11 games ahead of the defending champion Pistons and came within two games of tying Portland for the best record in the league. Yet as soon as the regular season ended, the Trail Blazers were made the favorites to win the NBA title.

Jordan won his fifth straight NBA scoring title with a 31.5 average and would be the league's Most Valuable Player once again. Scottie Pippen, who was on the verge of becoming a superstar in his own right, averaged 17.8 points a game, while Grant averaged 12.8. All three players were also outstanding defensively.

During the early rounds of the playoffs, Jordan was presented with the MVP prize. In his acceptance speech he told everyone what he really wanted.

"While I am very happy about receiving this award," he said, "I want a championship more. And I feel our chances are greater than they've ever been."

The playoff experience of the past several years began to show early. In the first round the Bulls went up against the New York Knicks. The Knicks were led by superstar center Patrick Ewing, but the team was just getting its playoff legs. It showed when the more experienced Bulls swept the Knicks in three straight games.

Next came the Philadelphia 76ers. Led by their great forward Charles Barkley, the Sixers had always played the Bulls tough. In fact, they held a 23-12 regular season edge over Chicago during the past seven years and had even beaten them three out of four in 1990–91. This could be the Bulls' first big test.

There were still skeptics throughout the league. Many felt the Bulls were still basically a one-man team. Reggie Miller of Indiana spoke for a lot of people when he said, "Trade Michael Jordan and what do they have? Nothing."

In reality, there was a great deal more pressure on the rest of the Bulls team. If they lost, no one would or could blame Jordan. He was a constant. If they won, well, then it was because they had perhaps the greatest player the game has ever known. Jordan's backcourt partner, John Paxson, explained some of the dilemma when he said:

"You have a player [Jordan] who can take over a game like nobody ever," Paxson said. "Yet you have one [also Jordan] who can get everyone involved. It's great to have a teammate like that, but try living up to it."

Not easy. The best way for the team to get the monkey off their backs would be to win. While Jordan might get the lion's share of the credit, knowledgeable basketball fans are well aware that no one player can bring a city a championship. Only a *team* can do that. One great player is just a bonus, especially if he can integrate himself into the team concept as Jordan obviously could.

The team had warmed up against the Knicks. In one of the games the Bulls had a 13-point lead when Michael went to the bench. When he returned, his teammates had jacked the lead up to 21. Games like that build confidence.

Against the Sixers, the Bulls won the first two at home easily. Back in Philly the Sixers squeaked out a two-point win in Game Three. The fourth game, also in Philadelphia, was pivotal. As it turned out, it might have also been one of the most pivotal games in Chicago Bulls history. It wasn't so much the final score. The Bulls won it, 101–85, excelling in offense and defense—and everybody contributed.

Jordan had 25 points, leading the team as usual. But Grant chipped in with 22 points and 11 rebounds, and Pippen scored 20 points while adding 9 rebounds and 5 assists. It was apparent that this was a different Chicago team than in the past. Even the players were aware of it, aware of past criticism and what they had to do.

"It's not easy when the media talk about us letting Michael down," said Horace Grant. "I used to sit there reading that stuff and thinking, 'Jeez, it's not like we're not trying.' But it has gotten easier, and this year has been the best of all."

With their newfound confidence, the Bulls eliminated the Sixers in five games, and for the third straight year would be facing the Detroit Pistons in the Eastern Conference finals. Would the Pistons be their Waterloo once again? At the outset the series was rated a toss-up. Some felt the experience and defensive pressure of the Pistons would prevail. Others felt the Bulls were the up-and-coming team. What happened surprised those on both sides of the fence.

The first game was close. Detroit was still in striking distance in the third period when reserves Craig Hodges and Cliff Levingston led a 13–7 run that upped the lead to nine points. From there the Bulls went on to win, 94–83. Call it a team win. It was just the beginning. Chicago went on to sweep the shocked Pistons in four straight games. The final was a 115–94 victory in which five Bulls were in double figures. Another team victory.

Now the team was in the championship round and awaiting the winner of the Western final between the Trail Blazers and Los Angeles Lakers. When the Lakers upset the Trail Blazers, that set up a matchup between Jordan and Lakers star Earvin "Magic" Johnson.

But there was more to it than that. The Lakers had won five NBA titles during the 1980s, and while they no longer had super center Kareem Abdul-Jabbar, they were a deep and experienced team. In Magic Johnson they had perhaps the greatest floor leader and point guard ever to play the game. Ever since he came into the league in 1979–80, Magic had been finding ways for his team to win. They won his first season when the 6'9" Johnson switched from point guard to center to replace the injured Abdul-Jabbar. In that game Magic responded with 42 points and 15 assists.

In addition, many teams fall short the first time they reach the championship round. The experience factor again. Besides Magic, the Lakers had a pair of experienced forwards in James Worthy and Sam Perkins, another veteran guard in Byron Scott and a young but improving center in Vlade Divac. The Lakers were made the early favorites by virtue of Magic Johnson's leadership and the team's championship experience.

The first game was close all the way, the lead changing hands a number of times. The Bulls felt they could run on the Lakers, who were an aging team and not very fast. They just couldn't get it going in the first one, though. The Lakers looked to slow things down, to play more of a half-court game. They were also doing a great deal of posting up on offense, playing with their backs to the basket and trying to work the ball in close to the hoop for high-percentage shots. The Bulls were having a tough time dealing with the strategy.

Chicago led by a 30–29 count after one quarter and 53–51 at the half. The fans at Chicago Stadium were waiting for their ballclub to put it in high gear and pull away. It wasn't happening. The Lakers continued to slow the pace and after three quarters had taken a 75–68 advantage. The fourth quarter was a battle all the way, just as it had been for the entire game. Finally the Bulls took a 91–89 lead and had the ball with 30 seconds left.

With the clock down below 25 seconds, Jordan missed a short jumper from the right side. The Lakers rebounded and moved downcourt. Magic had the ball and worked toward the hoop. He passed it back to Sam Perkins, who was open on the right side behind the three-point line. Perkins unleashed his left-handed jumper, and it went in for three! His clutch shot gave the Lakers the lead, 92–91, with 14 seconds left.

With nine seconds remaining, Jordan dribbled to the left side of the foul circle and put up a 17-footer. It kicked out. The Lakers' Byron Scott was fouled in the scramble for the loose ball and hit one of two free throws. Seconds later it was over, the Lakers winning 93–91.

Once again some of the old criticism surfaced. When Jordan missed a couple of key shots, the team lost. Pippen had 19 points in support of Jordan's 36, but they needed more. "I hope in the next game my supporting cast can hit some shots," Jordan said.

Again, he said it as a wake-up call. Jordan knew what had happened so often in the past, when his teammates tended to stand around and watch him do it. The Lakers were already favorites. If the Bulls lost the second game, they would face three more in L.A. already down 2-0. So the second game was perhaps the biggest in franchise history.

The Lakers also knew the Bulls couldn't win without a total team effort. Byron Scott put it this way: "If Jordan can go for 40 or 45 points and Pippen gets 17, that's okay. If Jordan is scoring that many points, it means the other guys aren't doing it."

It was Jordan himself who made a real effort to change things in the second game. He didn't come out shooting. Rather, he started feeding his teammates, passing the ball to them every chance he had. He put up just three shots in the first 18 minutes of the game. Would the strategy work?

Though the Bulls had a 48–43 lead at the half, the other players seemed to be responding. Horace Grant already had 14 points, and Paxson was hitting his jumper consistently. In the third quarter the Bulls finally opened it up. Jordan started to shoot more and go to the hoop, but his teammates kept contributing as well. Chicago scored 38 points in the third session and jumped to an 86–69 lead.

No one could call the Bulls a one-man team in 1991. Michael Jordan was still the biggest star, but now he had plenty of help. In championship-round action against the Lakers, Michael lobs a hook pass in the direction of teammate Stacey King. *(John W. McDonough photo)*

In the fourth the Bulls played out the 107–86 victory with complete confidence. They had shot 61.7 percent as a team. Jordan had 33, Grant and Pippen 20 each, while Paxson hit on all eight of his shots for 16 points. Defensively, the Bulls also stopped the Lakers. Magic Johnson, guarded mostly by Pippen, hit just 4 of 13 shots for 14 points.

Game Three in L.A. not only broke the tie, but it was further evidence that the Bulls now had the poise and talent to overcome adversity. It was a one-point game at the half, the Bulls ahead, 48–47. Then, in the midst of the third period, L.A. went on an 18–2 run that gave them a 67–54 lead. It would be easy for the Bulls to collapse. But Chicago fought back to reduce the lead to 72–66 after three. And they came back despite Jordan hitting just one of six shots in the period. A team effort again.

Midway through the fourth period the Bulls pulled even at 74. During the last eight minutes of action, eight different Bulls had scored. Jordan wound up hitting a last-second jumper to send the game into overtime, and in the five-minute extra session the Bulls came on to win it, 104–96. It gave them a 2-1 lead and further evidence that they could do it as a team.

After that Chicago just seemed to roll. They won the fourth game, 97–82, to take a 3-1 lead. And they were getting more respect from their opponents.

"I never dreamed this would happen," said Magic Johnson. "You anticipate a great series. You didn't anticipate anything like this. I can't feel bad because they're just giving us a nice butt-kicking."

By Game Five the Lakers were banged up and had to turn to a couple of younger players. They held off the Bulls heroically for most of the game, but Chicago was on a roll. In the final minutes the Laker defense tried to stop Jordan and Pippen from going to the hoop. So the Bulls began kicking the ball out to John Paxson, who hit three straight jumpers to put the game on ice. In fact, Paxson would score 10 points in the final 3:54 to help the Bulls to a 108–101 victory and a world championship.

To some, it might not rank as a huge upset. The Lakers had been favored, and Chicago had a bad habit of trying to let Michael Jordan do it all. If that had happened again, the Bulls wouldn't have won. At long last the other players on the team refused to allow it. Even Michael Jordan, the game's greatest player and playoff MVP, knew why the Chicago Bulls were champions.

"It was a seven-year struggle," he said. "We started from scratch, at the bottom, but every year we worked harder and harder, until we got it. Now we can get rid of the stigma of a one-man team. We did it as a team all season long. I played my game, but with their efforts, we were a better team."

There was little doubt about the Bulls now. Jordan was right. It had taken a long time, and when they finally won, it was still an upset.

As former NBA coach Mike Fratello explained, "Michael sacrificed as soon as his supporting cast blossomed. He's always been willing to spread the wealth around."

From the Bottom to the Top

Baseball has always been a game of records and statistics. When something new and exciting occurs on the diamond, the word spreads quickly. There are always comparisons to that which happened in the past. And when a new record is set, it is heralded all around the baseball world.

Great upsets don't always break records or set precedents. Yet there was one special upset-in-waiting, a precedent the baseball world had never seen. In fact, some said it would never happen because it was too much to expect from a group of athletes. Put simply, no big-league baseball team had ever gone from finishing in last place one year to winning the World Series the next. Taking it a step further, no team had ever gone from last place one season to winning a divisional title or even a pennant the next.

That's because a baseball team is the sum of all of its parts. For a team to finish last, there have to be problems with the pitching, or the hitting, or the defense. It's usually a combination of two or three of those elements. To fix them in one year is next to impossible. *Rebuilding* is the term used, and rebuilding takes time. As a rule, there is no quick fix.

The Minnesota Twins had been baseball's world champs in 1987. That year the Twins won their division with an 85-77 mark, not the kind of record that usually enables a team to finish first. In the playoffs they topped the Eastern Division winning Detroit Tigers in five games, then upset the favored St. Louis Cardinals in the World Series. The Twins won all four of their games in the Hubert H. Humphrey Metrodome, defeating the Cards, who took three at their home ballpark.

In 1987 Minnesota had some solid hitting with Kirby Puckett, Kent Hrbek, Gary Gaetti, and Tom Brunansky as a quartet of bona fide sluggers. Only Frank Viola and Bert Blyleven won more than 10 games among the pitchers, while Jeff Reardon was a top closer out of the pen. But the club was not deep and not a classic pennant and World Series winner.

Yet the team had another good year in 1988, winning 91 games but finishing far behind the Oakland A's in the American League West. Puckett hit .356 and drove home 121 runs, while Frank Viola won 24 games and the American League Cy Young Award. Then a year later the club started to falter, going 80-82, with a number of players having poor seasons. The most noticeable was Viola, who slumped to 8-12 and then was traded to the New York Mets for a trio of young pitchers near the end of the year.

Remember, no quick fix. In 1990 the Twins really began the slide. The young pitchers hadn't come on, and some of the veteran sluggers weren't hitting as they had in the past. The team was 42-46 shortly after midseason and 13½ games behind Oakland. But the pitching just wasn't there and it only got worse. Minnesota wound up at 74-87, in last place by a game and a half.

"You'd like to see guys pick each other up better than we have," said Manager Tom Kelly. "When Hrbek went into a slump in June, instead of guys rallying around him, they went into the tank with him. . . . Too many times we've gotten some runs on the board and then gone out and given it up."

The club really seemed to be in an eclipse. They had more errors (101) than home runs (100), and their homer total was the lowest since 1980. Even Kirby Puckett failed to hit a homer after July 15. To listen to Kent Hrbek, it would be several years before the Twins would be contenders again.

"We're in a rebuilding program, and we'll have to suffer through it," Hrbek said. "Hopefully, we'll develop the young pitchers before our veteran hitters start losing it."

Not a good prognosis. Then there were changes. Third sacker Gary Gaetti left the team via free agency. Shortly afterward, the Twins signed Jack Morris, the longtime pitching ace of the Tigers' staff. Morris was the winningest pitcher in the majors during the 1980s, but he was also 36 years old and coming off two losing seasons.

Veteran Mike Pagliarulo was signed to play third, and switch-hitting Chili Davis joined the team as a designated hitter. Much would still depend on the young pitchers—Scott Erickson, Rick Aguilera, Kevin Tapani, David West. The last three had come from the Mets in the Viola deal. Also on players like Puckett and Hrbek having big years with the bat.

The experts weren't convinced. A preseason poll of more than 180 members of the Baseball Writers' Association of America picked the Twins dead last. They were also the only American League team not to get a single, first-place vote. Another preseason article said this about Minnesota.

"The poor Twins," it read. "They will play their tails off and finish last. But in the process, they will continue their well-planned rebuilding program."

The only one who disagreed was manager Kelly. He was optimistic. "We're going to surprise some people," he said. "We've got some starting pitching. I've never had that before."

By the time the 1991 season was ready to open, the Twins had installed rookie Chuck Knoblauch at second and had another rookie, Scott Leius, platooning with Pagliarulo at third. There were a few more new players, as well, but once the season began, the Twins looked like another last-place disaster.

The team lost nine of its first 11 games. Morris was 0-3, Erickson and Allan Anderson were both 1-2, but in all fairness the pitchers were getting little support. The team batting average was .210. Left fielder Dan Gladden was struggling with a 1-for-21 start. Hrbek was 3-for-23, while Shane Mack, who had hit so well the season before, was 1-for-13. Only rookie Knoblauch, at 8-for-20, was hitting the ball well. Not surprisingly, with a 2-9 start, the team was once again in last place.

But their problems weren't something that a little heavy hitting wouldn't cure. Puckett, Chili Davis, and catcher Brian Harper all made major contributions with continuing help from rookie Knoblauch. The team won six of its next seven to keep from plunging farther into the basement. The winning streak also must have given them confidence, because they continued to play well. When they upped their record to 16-15, it marked the first time the ballclub had gone over the .500 mark since June 14, 1990.

They also had a hot pitcher. Right-hander Scott Erickson, who had pitched well the second half of 1990, was now pitching brilliantly. After seven decisions Erickson had a 5-2 record and a 1.45 earned run average. Though the season was still young, Erickson was being called the top hurler in the league. Yet after six weeks the team was still struggling to stay above .500 at 19-18. The encouraging part was that only a game and a half separated the Rangers, Angels, White Sox, and Twins in the American League West. The Twins trailed division-leading Oakland by just three and a half games.

The team continued to be an offensive force. Puckett, Knoblauch, and shortstop Greg Gagne were hitting over .300. DH Chili Davis was in the midst of a big comeback year with a .293 average and a team leading eight homers and 23 RBIs. The pitching was still spotty, and the club wasn't considered a contender by many people. But they were far from out of it, either.

By June 1 the Twins had slipped back to 23-25. A year earlier a 7-21 month of June all but finished the team for the year. A crucial 30-day period was about to begin, but catcher Brian Harper was optimistic.

"I don't think the same thing is going to happen this year," Harper said. "We know we're too good for that to happen again."

Harper was right. Only he hadn't gone far enough. Not only didn't the team slump, they suddenly caught fire. Two wins over Kansas City started it. Then came three straight over the Baltimore Orioles before three more over Cleveland. Suddenly the team had an eight-game win streak, their longest since 1985. They were also at 31-25 and in third place. These Twins were surely *not* a last-place team.

They still weren't finished. The whole team was hot. They buzzed through the Indians, Yanks, and Indians again during the next week, winning seven more times and running their winning streak to an amazing 15 games. It was the longest winning streak in the majors since the Royals had won 16 straight back in 1977. More important, the win streak had brought the Twins' record to 38-25 and to first place in the A.L. West. They led the A's by a half game.

One of the hottest of the Twins was pitcher Jack Morris, who had won six of his last seven starts with a 1.86 earned run average. Morris was happy to be in Minnesota, and his manager was happy to have him there.

A tough and tenacious competitor, pitcher Jack Morris loved pitching the big game. He was never better than in the seventh game of the 1991 World Series. *(AP/Wide World Photo)*

"We needed a guy like Jack," said Manager Kelly. "The last couple of years here, one pitcher would look at another and say, 'How about you taking care of it today?' Well, Jack takes care of it. And he takes the pressure off Erickson, Tapani, and the other young guys."

No one could call the Twins losers now. Their .278 team batting average was the best in the majors, while the pitching staff had a league low earned run average of 3.47. Some people began thinking the unthinkable. Could this team go from last place one year to a division title the next? Center fielder Kirby Puckett said he and his teammates were being careful not to become overexcited by their success.

"Most teams [with a 15-game win streak] would be jumping up and down," said Puckett. "Not us. We know this game can humble you."

While they were not getting overexcited, neither the Twins nor their opponents felt the Minnesotans would fold. "I think this team is, overall, much better than the '87 team," said utility infielder Al Newman, who was a member of both clubs.

Toronto scout Gordon Lakey was another who felt the Twins had a good shot at going from the bottom to the top. "The Twins are good," said Lakey. "They'll be a factor all year."

The streak ended with a 6–5 loss to the Orioles. But then the Twins showed their mettle. They regrouped almost immediately and won four of their next five. They now had a three-game lead over Oakland. Just before the All-Star break in July the team had a small letdown, dropping five of seven games. But they were 47-36 at the break and in a virtual tie for first with Texas.

"We have a chance to win this thing if we stay healthy and do things fundamentally right," said Manager Kelly.

At the All-Star break both Puckett and catcher Harper were over .300. Davis led the club with 19 homers and 52 runs batted in. Hrbek was at .281 with 42 ribbies. Erickson was at 12-3 with a 1.83 earned run average, while the veteran Morris was pitching well at 11-6. Rick Aguilera had 22 big saves out of the bullpen and had more than replaced the departed Jeff Reardon as the bullpen stopper.

Though the team forged back into first place after the All-Star Game, there were worries. The big one was Scott Erickson, who went on the disabled list with a sore elbow. The young right-hander had blown away the rest of the league in the first half, impressing everyone, including the veteran Morris.

"I've seen a lot of talented players who don't do anything in baseball because they don't have heart," said Morris. "Scott has heart. You can teach fundamentals and you can teach mechanics, but you can't teach heart. He's intense."

Erickson would return in about a week, but wasn't as dominant as he had been earlier in the year. Yet by July 21, the Twins had built a five-and-a-half-game lead over both Texas and Chicago. The team was now at 55-38. They were also picking each other up. If one or two players slumped, a couple more would get hot. Now Mike Pagliarulo and Shane Mack were on a tear.

By the first week in August the Twins were upsetting all the odds. They were 63-43 and had the best winning percentage in the entire major leagues. It was an incredible turnaround. On the mound, young Kevin Tapani had started pitching very well, running his record to 8-7. Erickson was 15-3 but still having some problems with his elbow. Overall, the team was gaining in confidence.

"I think we've proven now that we're for real," reliever Rick Aguilera said. "This isn't some fluke team in first place."

The race wasn't over yet. Now the White Sox

were on fire and challenging. On August 11 only one game separated the two teams, with Oakland three behind. Many figured the A's would eventually put it together and take their fourth straight division crown. It was the Twins who were still in first, though.

The difference was the other teams waxed hot and cold as the Twins continued to play consistent baseball. By August 25 Minnesota had a 75-51 mark and had opened up a seven-game lead over the White Sox and A's. In addition, they continued to have the best record in the majors.

In early September, with just a month to go, the Twins still led the majors with a .284 team batting average. Just about everyone was hitting. Among the pitchers, Erickson was at 16-6, Tapani at 13-7, and Morris at 16-10. Al Newman spoke of the position the team had worked so hard to achieve.

"We kind of have some leeway now," he said. "We're fortunate enough to be in a position where we can have a bad streak and still survive it."

In September the Twins simply held on to the lead. By September 15 the margin was seven and a half games over the White Sox. Minnesota seemed right on target to provide one of baseball's great upsets by going from the bottom to the top of their division.

At the 150-game mark the Twins were 90-60 and eight full games in front. Though they then lost six of eight, the lead was simply too great and the teams chasing them couldn't overcome it. Minnesota finished with a 95-67 record, winning their division by a comfortable, 8-game margin. They had gone from the bottom to the top, the first team in the history of baseball to do it.

"To do what we have done in the most extraordinarily competitive division in the history of baseball is one heck of an accomplishment," said general manager Andy MacPhail. "If you expected a team to be up by eight games with ten to play, you would have expected it to be Oakland, not us. To win it like we have is a credit to Tom Kelly and the players."

The team had a great year offensively. Puckett, Harper, Mack, and utility man Randy Bush all hit over .300. Davis, Puckett, Hrbek, and Mack were the top RBI men. Knoblauch hit .281 and would be American League Rookie of the Year. As for the pitchers, Erickson wound up at 20-8, Morris at 18-12, and Tapani at 16-9. A fine big three. Aguilera had 42 saves out of the pen, and there was some solid second-line pitching.

But before the playoffs began, baseball odds were upset again. In the National League West, the Atlanta Braves topped the Dodgers on the final weekend to take the division. Like the Twins, the Braves were a last-place team the season before. So something that had never been done in the history of the game had been done twice in one season. Now wouldn't it be something if one of the two teams could win the World Series?

In the playoffs the Twins had to face the Eastern Division winning Toronto Blue Jays. The championship series opened at the Metrodome, where the Twins took a 5–4 victory behind Jack Morris. In Game Two Blue Jays rookie Juan Guzman bested Kevin Tapani and the Jays won, 5–2. It was the first

Atlanta's Terry Pendleton was the National League's Most Valuable Player in 1991 and a major force in the playoffs and World Series. *(Courtesy Atlanta Braves)*

time the Twins had lost at home in seven postseason games going back to 1987.

Then Scott Erickson faced Jimmy Key in the important third game at the Sky Dome in Toronto. When Erickson gave up two quick runs in the first inning, Manager Kelly admitted he felt his team was in trouble.

"Sure, I was worried," he said. "If you get behind two-zip and your kid pitcher throws the ball 31 times in the first inning and you're trying to get through a best-of-seven series with just three starters like we are, then you'd be worried, too."

Erickson did settle down and pitched into the fifth, when David West replaced him. The Twins tied the game in the sixth, and it stayed that way through nine. Then, in the top of the 10th, Mike Pagliarulo smacked a clutch home run to give Minnesota a 3–2 lead, and Aguilera came on to close out the Jays in 1-2-3 fashion. The Twins were back on top, 2-1.

In Game Four the veteran Jack Morris took over. Always a great money pitcher with Detroit, Morris was again tough, going eight innings in a 9–8 Twins win. Minnesota was now one game away from going to the World Series for the second time in five years. They wanted to clinch in Toronto and then go home to await the winner of the Pittsburgh-Atlanta series in the National League.

The Blue Jays, however, built a 5–2 lead off Kevin Tapani by the fourth inning. In the sixth the Twins rallied again. Mack and Pagliarulo both singled. With Randy Tomlin relieving Tom Candiotti, one run came in on a fielder's choice, and then the tying tallies came home on a clutch double by Chuck Knoblauch.

It was knotted until the Minny eighth. With two out, Dan Gladden slapped a single and Knoblauch followed with a walk. Now Kirby Puckett was up facing lefty David Wells. Puckett dug in and slammed a double that scored Gladden and sent Knoblauch to third. The Twins now had a 6–5 lead. Moments later Kent Hrbek singled to drive home a pair of insurance runs and up the score to 8–5. The pennant was clearly theirs for the taking. Carl Willis retired the Jays in the eighth before Aguilera came on to close things out in the ninth. The Twins had won it in five games.

Kirby Puckett was the MVP of the playoffs, and when it was over he admitted that not even he thought the team would go from the bottom to the top.

"I'm not going to lie to you and say I thought we would win the American League pennant," he said. "I just knew that we wouldn't finish last again."

That they wouldn't. Now they were on their way to the World Series, and guess what? That other bottom-to-top team was there waiting for them. The Atlanta Braves had defeated the Pirates in seven games and would also be in the fall classic. Either way, baseball history would be made. One of the teams would be going from last place one year to World Champions the next. In a sense, it didn't matter which team won. It was already a season that produced a pair of the greatest upsets in baseball history.

The Braves had a fine team with an outstanding

pitching staff. It wouldn't be an easy series for the Twins. That's why they were happy it would open at the Metrodome. Everyone remembered how the Twins had taken all four games at home to become world champs in 1987. Maybe they could do it that way again.

It was certain that National Leaguers didn't like the Dome. Braves center fielder Ron Gant questioned the white roof, noting that outfielders have to follow a white baseball. Braves Manager Bobby Cox couldn't believe the playing surface.

"Their artificial surface is as hard as concrete," he said. "It's faster than anything in the National League. That means hard-hit ground balls can go all the way to the fence if your outfielders can't cut them off. Second, the banks of lights are lower than in outdoor stadiums, which means there are certain areas of the playing surface where your fielders can be blinded if the ball is hit on a low trajectory."

Jack Morris opened for the Twins, while Cox surprised everyone by picking veteran Charlie Leibrandt. Cox figured Leibrandt could show youngsters Tom Glavine, John Smoltz, and Steve Avery the way since he had pitched at the Dome when he was with the Royals. For two innings both veteran pitchers did the job. But in the third the Twins broke the ice when Knoblauch slashed a base hit to score Dan Gladden. 1–0.

In the fifth, the Twins really went to work. Hrbek doubled and Scott Leius singled. Then Greg Gagne KO'd Leibrandt by belting a three-run homer into the left-field seats. That made it a 4–0 game. Morris pitched into the eighth, when first Mark Guthrie, then Aguilera relieved him. The Braves tried to rally but wound up on the short end of a 5-2 decision.

Game Two saw Tapani facing Glavine. Minny took the lead in the first on a two-run homer by Chili Davis. Atlanta got one back in the top of the third and tied it in the fifth. It was still 2–2 in the bottom of the eighth. Young Scott Leius led off for the Twins. Leius had hit just five homers during the regular season, but now he took Glavine's pitch downtown to give the Twins a 3–2 lead. Aguilera came on to do his thing in the ninth and Minnesota had a two-game lead. And they were still unbeatable in World Series play at the Metrodome.

"We can't blame the ballpark or the umpires for this loss," said Atlanta Manager Bobby Cox. "We could have won with a clutch hit, but we didn't get one."

With the scene shifting to Atlanta for the third game, Minnesota went with Scott Erickson, hoping he could regain his first-half form. Atlanta countered with young southpaw Steve Avery, who had pitched extremely well in the playoffs. Minnesota took a 1-0 lead in the first, but then Atlanta began to chip away at Erickson. But by the time Manager Kelly pulled his starter for reliever Dave West in the fifth, Atlanta had taken a 4–1 lead.

A Puckett homer off Avery made it 4–2 in the seventh. Then in the Minny eighth, pinch hitter Brian Harper was safe on an error, prompting Manager Cox to remove Avery in favor of his closer, Alejandro Pena. With the righty Pena in the game, Manager Kelly sent up Chili Davis to pinch hit, and

Davis deposited one in the right-field seats, a two-run homer that tied the score.

After that the game became a stalemate, going into extra innings with both teams having opportunities, but neither able to score. In the top of the 12th Kelly even had to use pitcher Rick Aguilera as a pinch hitter. Aggie hit the ball hard, but it was gloved for an out. Both clubs were now running out of players rapidly.

Finally, in the bottom of the inning, the Braves rallied again. Dave Justice singled and, with one out, stole second. After a walk Mark Lemke slapped a single to left, scoring Justice with the winning run. The Braves were back in it. Both bottom-to-top teams were putting on quite a show. Then in Game Four it was the veteran Morris going for the Twins against young John Smoltz, the Braves' best pitcher the second half of the year. Smoltz had grown up in Detroit, and Morris had once been his idol.

"What I always remembered about Jack was his competitiveness," Smoltz said. "He went after each batter one hundred percent, no matter what the score. He battled you on every pitch, and that's the way I like to approach things now."

With both pitchers following the same philosophy, the game was tied at 1–1 into the seventh. Then the Twins took a 2–1 lead, and Kelly replaced Morris with Carl Willis in the bottom of the inning. Atlanta jumped on the reliever for a quick run to tie the game. It stayed 2–2 until the bottom of the ninth.

Mark Guthrie was now pitching for the Twins. With one out, the normally weak-hitting Mark Lemke blasted a triple. Righty Steve Bedrosian came in, and pinch hitter Jerry Williard hit a fly to medium right. Shane Mack caught the ball, and Lemke tagged at third, then headed for home. He slid in just ahead of the tag to score the winning run. The Series was now tied at two games each.

Kirby Puckett, for one, said his team wasn't ready to panic and reminded everyone about the great upset the team had provided just to make it to the fall classic. "We're still loose," Puckett said. "Remember, we're not even supposed to be here. Oakland is supposed to be here or maybe Chicago. Not us."

Kevin Tapani faced Tom Glavine in Game Five. This one wasn't even close. The Braves erupted for four in the fourth, six more in the seventh, and three in the eighth. When the smoke cleared, Atlanta had a 14–5 victory, pounding out 17 hits and scoring the most runs in a World Series game in 31 years. Suddenly the Twins had their backs against the wall.

Now they could only hope to duplicate 1987, when they won all four at the Metrodome. Game Six had Erickson opposing Avery. The Twins were worried because, as one scout said, Erickson had lost something since his midseason elbow problem.

"He just hasn't had the good pop since the elbow problem," said the scout. "He's gotten by some days because his ball moves well, but he's not anything special without that real hard sinker."

Even though neither pitcher was real sharp, the game was still close and hard-fought. Minnesota took an early 2–0 lead and staved off a Braves rally when Puckett made a spectacular leaping catch against the center field fence on a drive by Ron

Gant. But in the fifth the Braves finally tied it on a two-run homer by Terry Pendleton.

A Puckett sacrifice fly gave the Twins the lead in the bottom of the inning, but the Braves knotted it in the seventh, finally getting Erickson out of there. The righty had pitched a gutty game, keeping it close. It stayed a 3–3 game through nine, and once again it went into extra innings. Neither team could score and when Kirby Puckett stepped up to lead off the bottom of the 11th, he was facing lefty Charlie Leibrandt.

Puckett ran the count to 2–1 and then took Leibrandt's next pitch downtown, hitting a long home run to left field to win the game. Fans at the Metrodome went wild as Puckett circled the bases. His blast had not only saved the Twins, but it had also knotted the Series at 3-3, setting up a seventh and decisive game.

"I figured somebody had to step forward," Puckett said. "I've been here before. I was ready to let it stand out."

So once again it came down to a seventh game. The two teams that had both upset the odds and gone from last to first had put on a great show. In the finale it would be Morris against Smoltz once more. The veteran Morris couldn't wait to get his hands on the baseball.

"Let's get it on," he said before the game. "I don't know any pitcher who wouldn't look forward to a game like this. I don't feel any pressure, I'm relaxed. I've been in World Series games before, and I'm used to big games. It's something I enjoy."

The game would be a classic. Both pitchers were

A familiar scene to Minnesota Twins fans, center fielder Kirby Puckett getting a high-five from a teammate after a big hit. Puckett didn't disappoint, having a great playoff and World Series in 1991. *(AP/Wide World Photo)*

sharp and competitive. They simply refused to give in to the hitters. Each team had a couple of opportunities in the early going, but both Smoltz and Morris were at their best in the clutch. In both the sixth and seventh innings neither team could manage a hit, and the game was still scoreless. In fact, no seventh game of a World Series had ever gone scoreless for so long before.

In the eighth the Braves mounted a serious threat. Lonnie Smith led off with a single, followed by a long double by Terry Pendleton. But Smith hesitated rounding second and only made it to third. Had he kept running hard, he surely would have scored. Morris then bore down again. He got Ron Gant on a grounder, then walked Justice intentionally, loading the bases. Sid Bream then hit a hard grounder to Hrbek, who started a nifty 3-6-3 double play. The Twins had dodged another bullet.

Then, in the bottom of the inning, Minnesota loaded the sacks with one out. Lefty Mike Stanton was pitching for the Braves with Hrbek up. The big first sacker slammed a hard liner toward second. But Mark Lemke took two quick steps to his right, gloved it, then stepped on second for an unassisted double play. Both teams had now missed golden opportunities, and the tension mounted.

It remained scoreless through the ninth. For the third time in the Series a game went into extra innings. Surprisingly, Morris came out to pitch the 10th. The gritty veteran had refused to come out of the game. Still the ultimate competitor, Morris retired the Braves in order, 1-2-3. The fans gave him a standing ovation as he left the field.

Pena was pitching for the Braves as Dan Gladden led off the bottom of the inning. Gladden waited on a fastball and promptly slammed a broken-bat double to left. Knoblauch then bunted him over to third. Manager Cox ordered Puckett and Hrbek walked intentionally, loading the bases and setting up a possible double play. Lefty-swinging Gene Larkin then came up as a pinch hitter.

"I went up there with two ideas in my head," Larkin said. "Get a strike and hit it in the air. I knew a fastball was coming because that's all Pena really throws. I was ready."

Sure enough, Larkin got the fastball on the first pitch, and sure enough, he hit it in the air. As soon as he hit it, he thrust his fist into the air and trotted toward first. Watching the ball from third, Gladden also threw his fist skyward. Right fielder Brian Hunter, who was playing shallow to try to cut the run off, took two steps back, then stopped. He watched the ball drop behind him as Gladden trotted home with the run that won the World Series. The Twins were again the world champs by virtue of a great 1–0 victory in Game Seven, completing their unlikely odyssey.

Though the Twins were officially champs, there really wasn't a loser. Both clubs had upset all the odds and made baseball history. They then went out and played one of the greatest World Series ever. As the Braves' Terry Pendleton put it:

"I can't remember a Series where every pitch, every inning, every strike, every out mattered so much," he said. "When I came up in the tenth inning of the last game, I was talking to Brian Hunter. He said, 'Why don't we just quit now and call it a tie.' "

Maybe that would have been best, but baseball doesn't work that way. There has to be a winner, and in 1991 it was the Minnesota Twins. Not only were they winners and world champs, but they were a team who had pulled off one of the most monumental upsets ever. Ask the oddsmakers? At the beginning of the year no one thought the Twins could possibly win. But they did—and so did the Braves. Last to first. It had never happened before. Leave it to baseball to have it happen twice in the same year.

Jimbo's Open

He came roaring out of Belleville, Illinois, in the early 1970s, and in doing so changed the face of tennis forever. Of all the major sports, tennis was perhaps the furthest removed from the mainstream. The sport was long on elegance and etiquette. Both players and crowds were dignified and courteous. Though many of the great players had a burning desire to win, they usually kept it inside them, rarely vocalizing, rarely showing their emotions. Most players used the same basic form on their strokes and played what was known as a serve-and-volley game.

Then James Scott Connors came along. Jimmy for short. Jimbo later on. He not only brought with him the brash, cocky street-fighter temperament usually seen in other sports, but also a new style and a way of playing the game that baffled the tennis establishment and immediately spawned a whole slew of imitators.

Connors was a southpaw slugger. In a game that often relied on a big serve, then a rush to the net to volley (take the ball on the fly) the return, Connors often stayed back near the baseline. While other players relied on placement and spin, Connors used power. He blasted every ball as hard as he could.

Up to that time, almost all players held their racket in one hand, hitting both their forehand and backhand that way. Connors brought something else to the game. He hit his backhand shots with both hands on the racket. Using the two-hand backhand, Connors looked like a baseball player swinging for the fences—and he always tried to hit a home run.

He won his first tournament in 1972, when he was not yet 20 years old. By the end of 1973 he was ranked third in the world. Then, a year later, James Scott Connors took the tennis world by storm. He started by winning the Australian Open, the first of his eight grand-slam championships. Next came Wimbledon, the all-English championships.

Playing on the fast grass courts that are supposedly tailored for the serve-and-volley specialists, Connors blasted one opponent after another into submission. Then, in the final, he met the great Australian veteran, Ken Rosewall. Rosewall was in his late thirties, past his prime, but still a dangerous player with one of the best backhands in the game. But against Jimmy Connors, he looked like a helpless child.

Connors came out swinging. He emitted loud

A youthful Jimmy Connors played a power game that blasted opponents into submission. Jimbo would not change his basic game despite advancing years. *(Courtesy United States Tennis Association)*

grunts on every shot and blasted one winner after another past the hapless Rosewall. When it ended, Jimmy had an easy 6-1, 6-1, 6-4 triumph and was the new king of the tennis world.

Connors completed his great 1974 season in the fall by winning the first of his five U.S. Open championships. Once again he met the veteran Rosewall in the final and again demolished him. This time the scores were 6-1, 6-1, 6-0. It was the beginning of a new era. At year's end Jimmy Connors was the number one–ranked men's player in the world. He would be number one for the next five years.

During that time Connors's presence on the tennis scene was well known. Besides his obvious skills, his behavior was sometimes questioned by tennis purists. He would often vocalize during a match, talking to himself and not hiding his emotions. At times he would argue calls vehemently, chastising umpires and linesmen if he felt they had made errors. He would celebrate winning a tough point by pumping his fists back and forth or making other gyrations.

The crowds soon began taking sides. They either loved him or hated him—but wherever Jimmy Connors played, he stirred emotions. This was something tennis had often lacked. Though Connors would win only one more Wimbledon after 1974, he would always make the U.S. Open his own personal stage. The Open was always his favorite tournament because the New York crowds were more vocal than most and could identify with the street-fighter mentality that Connors brought to center court.

He would win the Open five times, his last title coming in 1983. In addition, he would lose a pair of finals and also half a dozen semifinals. He was always in the thick of the Open action, giving the crowds a great show. While Jimbo remained near the top of the rankings in the early- to mid-1980s, he slowly stopped winning the big ones.

First Bjorn Borg, then John McEnroe, and finally Ivan Lendl took over the number-one spot. But Connors never stopped fighting or giving it his all on the court. His love of tennis was obvious. He played as often as he could, and by the mid-1980s had won more tournaments (more than 100) than any player in history.

Toward the late 1980s Connors was moving into his midthirties, and more powerful young players kept coming into the game. But Jimmy kept battling them. While other veteran players left the sport, citing something akin to burnout, Jimmy Connors continued to play.

"I play because I make a heck of a living and have a darn good time," Connors commented back in 1984.

Though he now admitted that he hated spending so much time away from his wife and two children, he still refused to discuss retirement. "My boy knows what I do for a living," he said. "My little girl, a little bit, but not to the point of really understanding. It's difficult on everybody, but it is the way I make a living."

More and more, Connors showed flashes of his old self. If younger players could get him into a long match, a four- or five-setter, they knew there would be a chance he would run out of gas. At Wimbledon in 1988 the 35-year-old Connors played a long five-setter in the third round, defeating American Derrick Rostagno, 7-5, 4-6, 4-6, 6-4, 7-5.

He came back from a two-set-to-one deficit to win it, prompting Rostagno to comment: "Tennis is an art and Jimmy Connors is an artist. It was thrilling."

Then in the fourth round he got himself into another five-setter, losing to a West German named Patrick Kuhnen, who was nearly 14 years younger. After the match Kuhnen noted that Jimmy "never gives up. He's the biggest fighter."

But more and more it was looking as if the end was near. In 1990 Connors had to have reconstructive surgery on his left wrist. There were rumors he might not come back. But he did. Now he said he was just playing for fun, for the love of the game and to "see what I can do against some of these young kids." He wasn't even ranked in the top 100.

He entered the French Open, a tournament he had never won because the slow, red-clay courts at Roland Garros Stadium were far from his favorite surface. Surprisingly, he got into a classic match with young Michael Chang that had the crowd on its feet. Again trailing by 2-1 in sets, Jimbo battled back from the brink of defeat to win the fourth set and tie the match. But with the crowd solidly behind him, Connors walked slowly to the referee and told him he had to default, that he couldn't continue. He was totally exhausted, his body cramping up.

When the ref asked him if he was sure, Connors said, "I've been playing my tail off for four sets. Don't you think if I could continue, I would?"

His default to Chang grabbed the headlines. He still could cut it on the court, but Father Time and the physical grind of a long match were obviously catching up to him. Then in September it was U.S. Open time again. Connors was 39 years old, and in the eyes of many his 5'10", 155-pound body was wearing down. He was ranked just 174th in the world. But coming to the National Tennis Center at Flushing Meadows in Queens (one of the five boroughs of New York City) always seemed to give Jimmy Connors new life.

"I've always loved playing here," Connors said. "It never mattered if they [the fans] were for me or against me. I think, more importantly, that people still get charged up when I come out to play. I know I still get charged up."

The question was how much time would he have to get fully charged. Connors's first-round opponent was Patrick McEnroe, the younger brother of John, but a talented and improving player. He was heavily favored to end Connors's 1991 Open almost as soon as it began. For nearly three sets it looked as if he would.

Playing confidently and hitting with great accuracy, McEnroe won the first set, 6-4. Connors was also playing well, especially for a guy ranked 174th in the world, but McEnroe just seemed a tad better. The second set was close all the way. It finally went to a seven-point tiebreaker, and McEnroe prevailed again. He took the second set, 7-6, and was one set away from sending Connors packing.

When Jimbo fell behind 3-0 in the third set, the match appeared over. No one could blame Connors if he simply played out the string and went home. But perhaps they had forgotten the competitive fires that burned inside James Scott Connors. They had never been extinguished and probably never would. Connors knew only one way to play, and that was as hard as he could. And he never stopped fighting

Mention the U.S. Open and Jimmy Connors's eyes light up. The Open has always been his tournament, and in 1991 he delighted the fans perhaps as never before. *(Courtesy ATP Tour)*

until the final point of the match was won, either way.

McEnroe was serving in Game Four. He took a 40–0 lead, one point from winning yet another game and just nine points from the match. Suddenly Jimmy Connors dug down to perhaps a place that even he had never been before. He narrowed his eyes and looked across the net at the confident McEnroe. He knew in his heart he was not yet beaten, and he promptly blasted McEnroe's next serve back for a winner.

Remarkably, Connors rallied to win the game. He was still way behind, but it was a beginning. His next step was to salvage the set, which he did, taking five of the next six games to win it, 6-4. From there his uphill battle continued. When he won the fourth set, 6-2, to even the match, the crowd roared its approval. They were getting just what they wanted. By then it was the old Connors, exhorting himself on every big point and in doing so drawing the crowd deeper and deeper into the match—into the match on his side.

Many, however, remembered what happened against Chang in the French Open, that Jimbo rallied to tie the match at two sets apiece, then had to default because of exhaustion. Could he make it through a fifth set?

But this was the U.S. Open. Connors loved playing here. If there was anything left in his 39-year-old body, he would find it. And sure enough he did, continuing to play brilliant tennis in the fifth set. His two-handed backhand was still a deadly shot, finding the corners, whistling crosscourt, and helping him win the day.

When it ended, Connors had a 6-4 fifth-set victory. He had come back all the way to win the four-and-a-half-hour marathon. It ended at 1:35 A.M., and the fans remaining at the stadium went absolutely nuts as Connors thrust his index finger in the air to indicate that he had won one more time.

As miraculous as Connors's win had been, it was too much to hope for any more. After all, he had already upset the odds by coming back against McEnroe. Yet he had to continue. His next match was against Michael Schapers, and he won easily, 6-2, 6-3, 6-2. This may have been the only match in the tournament when Jimbo wasn't the underdog.

His next opponent was a big, strong Czech named Karel Novacek. Many felt Novacek would wear Connors down with his power. Instead it was Jimbo, hitting winners and perhaps even intimidating Novacek somewhat by his dynamic presence, that once again had the crowd firmly on his side. Jimbo won the match, 6-1, 6-4, 6-3. He was still alive.

Now he had to prepare for another tough match, this one against the talented Aaron Krickstein. Krickstein played a lot like Connors, preferring long rallies from the baseline to volleying at the net. As a consequence, he often played long, exhausting matches with the potential to go the full five sets. Krickstein's stamina was always one of his strong points. It was hard to imagine Jimbo lasting through another five-setter and coming out on top. Injuries had often prevented Krickstein from achieving his true potential. When healthy, he was close to a top-10 player, and as a consequence he came into the match as an overwhelming favorite.

As expected, the 24-year-old Krickstein came out fast, trying to move Connors from side to side. You get an older player running early, and the legs might fail him late. Everyone going against Connors remembered what had happened in the French Open, but this was New York, the place where Jimmy Connors loved to perform. So even when Krickstein won the first set, 6-3, the fans had hope. Maybe Jimbo could do it again, pull off yet another miracle.

In the second set the match began to tighten up. Connors was playing well, starting to control more of the rallies and not running quite so much. He was also taking a lot of time between points, toweling off. The rules say a player has to be ready for the next point in 25 seconds. Connors sometimes took as much as 40.

Chief of umpires Jay Snyder said a big reason was the crowd. "There was just no way play could have been resumed in 25 seconds with the crowd as excited as it was," he said.

The match continued. The second set went to a tiebreaker, and Connors dug down to win it. So he had evened the match by taking the second set, 7-6. Then, in the third set, Connors suddenly seemed to lose it. He looked all of his 39 years as Krickstein breezed, 6-1. Once more Jimbo was down 2-1 in sets, and it would take a five-set match for him to win it.

Connors continued to look for every advantage. He whipped the crowd into a frenzy, sometimes stalled for time, argued just enough with the officials to make sure they watched extra hard. Through it all he also continued to play amazing tennis. He came back to take the fourth set, 6-3, sending the match to a decisive fifth.

Then Krickstein began to dominate again. He was winning the key points and broke Connors's serve twice to take a 5-2 lead. He was just one game away from the match, but still Jimmy Connors refused to quit. For a player his age to come back from 5-2 in a match that was already over the four-hour mark seemed impossible. But here came Connors, defying the odds and turning back the clock once more. He broke back and began to dominate the match. Incredibly, he battled back to the point where the final set was tied at six games each. Now a seven-point tiebreaker would decide the winner.

Breathing hard and sometimes gasping for breath between points, Connors continued to blast away at the ball. With each point he won, the crowd roared its approval, pumping Connors up even more. When he won the tiebreaker, 7-4, the National Tennis Center erupted. Once again Jimbo turned slowly around, holding up his index finger to the entire crowd. One more match, he indicated, was under his belt.

By this time Jimmy Connors was the talk of the whole tournament. His old opponents, many of them long since retired, admired his grit. "What Jimmy has," said former star Ilie Nastase, "is what we all would kill for. Just one more time."

Even defending champ Pete Sampras knew that no matter what happened, nothing could erase the hysteria over Jimmy Connors. "It's Jimmy's tournament now, no matter what happens," said Sampras.

Connors himself couldn't quite explain what was happening. When an interviewer would ask him how he was doing it, Jimbo would just smile in a half-cocky, half-quizzical way.

"I can't really explain what's happening here," he would say. "I don't really know what to expect out of myself anymore. Sometimes it doesn't seem real. You've almost got to laugh at it. Imagine me beating these young guys."

You knew that Connors was loving every minute of it. So were some of the younger players, especially the ones who didn't have to meet Connors.

"How can you not like what Jimmy is doing," said French Open champ Jim Courier. "He's great for the game."

Courier had something else at stake. He and Jimbo were on a collision course to meet in the semifinals if each could win one more match. In the quarter finals Connors would be meeting Paul Haarhuis of the Netherlands. No one expected Haarhuis to get this far, but the youngster from Eindhoven was playing especially well and was fresh off an upset of his own. He had defeated the outstanding young German, Boris Becker. Now he had his sights on Jimmy Connors.

Haarhuis started out full of confidence in the first set. He was playing virtually error free, hitting the ball hard and making deft placements from both the forehand and backhand sides. Again it was hard to see Connors holding him off. Haarhuis won the first set, 6-4. Under ordinary circumstances this should have given the Dutchman a real shot of confidence, but like everyone else, he knew what Connors had done thus far in the tournament.

Haarhuis, however, continued to play well. He got a service break in the second set, and then, with the score at 5-4, he would be serving to win it. Again, Connors battled. Jimbo finally had the advantage and was a point away from tying the set. Then came a remarkable point in which Connors returned four straight overhead smashes from Haarhuis. Jimmy then blasted a backhand down the line to win the point and sent the crowd into a frenzy once more. He was at it again.

When he won the set in a tiebreaker, he had effectively broken Haarhuis's will. The youngster didn't have the experience to cope with the Connors mystique and the roaring New York crowd. Jimbo won the final two sets, 6-4 and 6-2 to take the match. Incredibly, he was in the semifinals.

Now Jimbo was psyched. He repeated again that he couldn't explain his success and that he was just going one match at a time. But he was one of just four players left in the tournament. In the eyes of many New Yorkers, this was where Jimmy Connors belonged. He was joined by three of the world's best players—Courier, the number-one seed Stefan Edberg, and the three-time Open champion Ivan Lendl. Connors had come in ranked 174th! It was truly an upset of monumental proportions, no matter what happened.

Perhaps the essence of Jimmy Connors's attitude about the U.S. Open came when he was told that after losing, defending champ Sampras said that he felt a bag of bricks had been lifted from his shoulders. Hearing this, Connors almost flew into a rage.

"How can he say that!" exclaimed Jimbo. "Being the U.S. Open champion is what I've lived for. If these guys are relieved at losing, something is wrong with the game."

Sampras was still a very young player who might not have even realized what he was saying. But it struck a chord in Connors, who had known only one way to play since he came out of Belleville nearly two decades earlier.

In the semifinals against Courier, Connors finally met his match. The 21-year-old Courier, who had been compared to Connors in talent and temperament, had just too much power for the old man. Courier was on his game and didn't rattle when Connors excited the crowd with an occasional brilliant shot. Courier just went about his business and won the match easily, 6-3, 6-3, 6-2. Jimbo's run was over, but it would not be forgotten.

Even when Stefan Edberg played an absolutely brilliant match to top Courier for the title, it was Jimmy Connors who continued to dominate the conversation.

"Jimmy is Mr. Open," said the champion Edberg. "He really gave the tournament a boost, and for that I thank him. He let me sneak in the back way."

Edberg knew that Jimmy Connors would be the

Many feel that Jim Courier will emerge as the best player in the 1990s. Often compared to Connors, it was Courier who ended Jimbo's string of fantastic upsets by beating him in the semifinals of the 1991 U.S. Open. *(Courtesy ATP Tour)*

talk of New York. But Jimbo was still hard-pressed to explain his success, and he still refused to talk about retirement. He even hinted that his game might improve more because he was still coming back from the wrist surgery of a year earlier.

One thing, however, was very apparent. Jimmy

Connors, the street fighter from Illinois, still loved the game of tennis, still loved to compete, and loved to upset players 10 or 15 years his junior. That was never more apparent than at the 1991 U.S. Open. Jimmy Connors didn't win the tournament, but his great upsets made him as much a champion as in those years when he actually held the championship trophy high over his head, forever playing to the New York crowd that had made him one of their own.

About the Author

BILL GUTMAN has been an avid sports fan ever since he can remember. A freelance writer for twenty years, he has done profiles and bios of many of today's sports heroes. Mr. Gutman has written about all of the major sports and some lesser ones as well. In addition to profiles and bios, he has also written sports instructional books and sports fiction. He is the author of Archway's *Sports Illustrated* series; *Great Sports Upsets; Bo Jackson: A Biography; Pro Sports Champions;* and *Michael Jordan: A Biography,* available from Archway Paperbacks. Currently, he lives in Poughquag, New York, with his wife, two stepchildren, and a variety of pets.

Don't Miss a Single Play!

Archway Paperbacks Brings You the Greatest Games, Teams and Players in Sports!

By

Bill Gutman

☆ Baseball's Hot New Stars...........68724-7/$2.75

☆ Football Super Teams.................74098-9/$2.95

☆ Great Sports Upsets...................70925-9/$2.75

☆ Pro Sports Champions...............69334-4/$2.75

☆ Bo Jackson: A Biography..........73363-X/$2.95

☆ Michael Jordan: A Biography....74932-3/$2.99

☆ Baseball Super Teams.................74099-7/$2.99

☆ Great Sports Upsets 2.................78154-5/$2.99

All Available from Archway Paperbacks

Simon & Schuster Mail Order
200 Old Tappan Rd., Old Tappan, N.J. 07675

Please send me the books I have checked above. I am enclosing $_____(please add $0.75 to cover the postage and handling for each order. Please add appropriate sales tax). Send check or money order–no cash or C.O.D.'s please. Allow up to six weeks for delivery. For purchase over $10.00 you may use VISA: card number, expiration date and customer signature must be included.

Name _____

Address _____

City _____ State/Zip _____

VISA Card # _____ Exp.Date _____

Signature _____

630

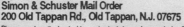